AUSTIN

LINDA FORD

1

Late 1887

Austin Wagoner reined in at the sound of gunshots. Several shots, which meant it couldn't be someone killing an animal. Or shooting a snake, though likely all the snakes had gone to their dens for the winter. In fact, it sounded like several shooters were involved.

Austin looked toward the west. He'd like to be safe in his cabin before a winter storm made travel challenging, if not impossible.

But he was almost certain what the shots meant. The stage was being robbed. He'd overheard stories of a large payroll being on board. Whether it was true or simply idle gossip, it seemed likely he wasn't the only one who'd heard the news.

He had to see if he could be of help. He'd put his guns away for good. Again. Hoping this time it would be permanent. Only a call for help from an old friend had persuaded Austin to leave his mountain retreat where he'd spent two winters and planned to spend another. He'd hung his beloved bowler hat on a nail in the cabin his friend had provided, knowing it was like a sign around his neck announcing Auss the gunman. He'd gone to Fort Macleod to stock up on supplies. His tweed jacket—another of his trademarks—had been replaced by a shearing-lined coat.

With a weary sigh, he pulled his gun belt from his pack, buckled it around his hips and tied the holster around his leg. It informed everyone that he was a gunman, but it also ensured he could get his gun out in good time. He pulled his cowboy hat more securely on his head and then galloped over the hill, the packhorse following reluctantly, slowing Austin's pace. They reached the road and raced onward. The shots had stopped. Maybe whatever the cause, it was over and he was no longer needed. But he didn't rein in his horse. He wouldn't resume his journey until he was certain he couldn't be of help.

Around the next corner, he saw four men kicking through goods scattered over the ground. Tracks down the embankment informed Austin that the coach had gone over the edge. One of the men glanced up, saw him approaching and the four of them hastened to mount up and ride away.

Austin stopped at the site. He hurried to the two men stretched out on the ground. Presumably the driver and the shotgun rider. They had breathed their last. He glanced over the goods strewn around. Women's garments. Smaller clothing for children. Travelers on the coach?

Something on the ground flashed. Was it a coin? He picked it up and stared, his mouth suddenly slack.

A golden heart on a chain. Engraved on the heart were the initials A and M, intertwined like they were one. He'd thought of two people becoming one when he'd had the locket made.

How was it possible? And yet, there was no mistaking the evidence he held in his hand. He'd given this locket to Mae five years ago. Not many days before he last saw her.

Mae! Had she been on the coach or had she sold the heart or maybe given it away?

He peered over the edge of the embankment. The stage lay on its side, tipped toward the embankment, one wheel broken. The horses were gone. He looked both ways and saw no evidence of the missing animals. He returned his attention to the scene below him. Did he detect a movement inside the coach?

"Hello?" He waited. No answer but he was certain he saw the top of a head in the curtainless window.

But of course, whoever was down there had no way of knowing if he was one of the robbers.

"Hello. I've come to help." Several waiting seconds. "Is there someone down there?"

A head popped up in the window and disappeared as if the body had been snatched back or fallen but Austin was sure of what he'd seen. A boy. A towheaded boy.

There was nothing for it but to investigate. He could backtrack several miles to find a suitable way down or…

He grabbed up the reins of both horses, led them to the nearby trees, left them to graze then began the descent. He started out on his heels, but seconds later he was on his backside, grabbing at every bit of brush to slow his downward path.

He skidded to a halt, righted himself, and jumped to the upturned side of the stage to look in the door.

That's when he saw her.

Mae.

His lungs struggled. From the speed of coming down the hill. Or so he told himself. But seeing Mae again sent shock waves through his heart.

Five years had only made her more beautiful. She'd gone from a dewy-eyed eighteen-year-old to a confident-looking, mature young woman. Her thick blonde hair, which she always struggled to keep neat, was in complete disarray. Her high cheekbones were pale.

Her eyes, which he'd always said were blueberry in color, were wide and unfocused. She wore a slate gray traveling outfit—a slim skirt and matching jacket against the cold. She clung to a little girl and tugged on the shirttail of a younger boy who stared at him with a combination of fear and challenge.

He shifted his attention back to Mae.

"Mae Martyn. I'd recognize you anywhere." She gave no sign of answering. "Perhaps you aren't Miss Martyn any longer." In five years, she could have been courted and wedded several times. But it wasn't long enough to have children this age. "Are any of you hurt?" He edged closer, needing to assess the situation but moving cautiously as he recognized the shock in three sets of eyes.

Mae blinked. "Children, are you all right?" She ran her gaze over the girl, then over the boy.

"I'm okay," the boy said.

The girl sucked in a shuddering breath but gave no other answer.

At the children's reactions, Mae seemed to shake herself and bring her thoughts to their situation.

"Austin, imagine seeing you here." Her tone was more dismissive than surprised. More critical than grateful. Not that he could blame her. He knew she wouldn't want to ever see him again. But he was all she had at the moment.

The girl swallowed audibly and clung to Mae. "Those men…"

"They're gone," Austin assured her. He waited a minute, but Mae seemed disinclined to introduce him. "My name is Austin Wagoner. I'll help you all get to safety."

He again waited. Nothing. Shock must have driven rational thought from them all.

"And who do we have here?" he asked.

The boy responded first. "I'm Colin Martyn. I'm eight." He puffed up his chest as if that age made him all grown up.

Surprise ran up and down the length of Austin's body. Colin Martyn was dead. He'd seen it with his own eyes. Felt it in the burning depths of his heart. Besides, Colin had been a full-grown man. Then his reason took hold. This was Colin's son. For some reason, Austin thought he'd still be a baby. He studied the boy. Towheaded, brown eyes like his father. But that was the only similarity he saw. Beneath the brown woolen coat, Austin could see that the boy's shirt was twisted. One pant leg was up to his knee. Austin could only guess that the three of them had endured a wild ride down the slope.

Colin indicated the others. "She's my sister, Rosie. And my Aunt Mae."

He remembered Rosie as a pretty little girl, who talked non-stop. Her hair was a darker blonde than either her aunt or brother. She had eyes a paler blue than Mae's. Unlike her brother, her clothes—a pretty blue dress and a dark gray coat—were neat.

He realized he was staring and made himself stop. "Pleased to meet you all. Now let's see what we can do about getting you out of here. Colin, you first." The boy had already climbed up the seat as far as he could. Austin reached for the boy who took his hand. He pulled him from the coach. They stood on the side of the conveyance. Higher than the height of a man. "Wait on the ground."

Colin clambered down the side of the coach and stood looking up.

"Who's next?" Austin asked.

"I can manage on my own." Struggling against the constraints of her skirt, Mae pulled herself up and perched beside him. She turned to the girl. "Come on, Rosie."

Rosie scrambled from the coach. The pair stared at the ground below, then Mae lowered herself over the edge, hung there, her feet swinging as she searched for a foot hold. It was two more feet to the ground.

Seeing her problem, Austin jumped down and reached up to take her around the waist.

She kicked at him. Her fingers slipped and she landed in his arms with enough force to drive him backward and her into his chest.

"Let me go!"

He did so with haste. "My apologies. I was only trying to help." Before Mae could express her feelings, he gently lowered Rosie to the ground.

He faced the three of them. "Are you sure none of you are hurt?"

Colin and Rosie nodded. Mae looked at him with cool disdain.

He'd take that as a yes.

"We slid down the hill," Colin said. "Never even turned over once."

"Cause Auntie prayed," Rosie said, her voice quivering.

Austin studied the coach, then returned to face the trio. "The wheel next to the back is shattered. Might be what kept you from rolling. That and God," he added hastily, lest any of them think he meant to take any credit from the Heavenly Father.

Mae sprang into action. "Where are our things? We need them."

"There's luggage up the hill," Austin said. He might possibly be able to scramble up there and retrieve the belongings. He studied the bank he'd slid down. Somehow he didn't fancy dragging the others up there.

"Auntie, the box of books is still here." Colin pointed toward the nearby crate. "Didn't even bust open. Guess you nailed it real good. And our trunk is still strapped to the top."

"Good, but where are our valises? We need our clothing to go on." Mae sounded like someone, or something, should get their belongings in order.

Rosie shivered. Her breathing stuttered.

Austin recognized the signs of shock. It could be the girl had injuries she was unaware of.

There was a blanket nearby. He picked it up and draped it over the little girl's shoulders. He thought Mae might be feeling shock, too, but didn't venture to wrap the blanket over her. "Sit and rest while I assess the situation." He guided Rosie toward the crate Colin had mentioned and she sank to it.

Mae moved to the girl's side.

Austin studied them a moment. He'd keep an eye on the three of them in case there was a delayed reaction. In the meantime, he had to come up with a plan to get them out of there.

Colin studied him. "How come you know my aunt?"

"I knew her a few years ago. I even knew you though you were pretty little."

"How little?"

"Well, let me think. Seems to me you were running around." He chuckled. "And talking. Yup. As I recall, your favorite word was 'more.'"

"More what?"

"More everything. More food. More play. More horsey rides. I used to swing you on my foot. That was your horsey ride." Bittersweet memories crowded his mind. He blinked and focused his attention on the coach. It was relatively undamaged. Hard to believe it had fallen down the hill. But it did not offer a way of transportation.

"Did you know my mama and papa," the boy asked.

"I did. How's your mama?"

"Dead. I don't hardly remember her. It's just me and Rosie and Auntie."

Dead? He didn't know. Hadn't heard. But then he'd ridden away and never looked back. Didn't seek any news of his past. "I'm sorry to hear that. So where are you headed?"

"Auntie has a new job as a teacher on a ranch."

"I see." So she'd become a teacher just as she planned. What other plans of hers had been fulfilled or shattered? He wouldn't dwell on the question. Any right he'd once had to know things about her no longer existed.

"I think it's called the Circle A Ranch."

"I know of the place." He'd rescued a man and woman and two small boys who were stranded in the mountains. They were headed for the Circle A. He wondered how they were doing now.

"We need to get on with our journey," Mae spoke from behind him.

He'd been keenly aware of her leaving Rosie's side and closing the distance separating them. Huh. There was far more than the space of a few feet between them. There was a gulf as deep as the earth itself.

He turned slowly to face her. Felt again the jar of recognition and the flash of memories. "How do you propose to do that?" Let her figure out they were without transportation.

She looked at the coach, moved her gaze to the empty rigging, swept it up the hill, then back to him and released a long, long sigh. "I don't suppose there are horses up there or another stage coach."

"Just my two horses and one is a pack animal."

Her eyes were wide, her gaze steady. She brushed her hair back from her face. "How far is it to the nearest place?"

He looked to his left. "Fort Macleod is back there. About two hours away." He shifted his gaze to the right. "Logan Crossing is about two hours that way. From there you could get a ride to the Circle A Ranch." He paused. Was she as stubborn now as she'd been in the past? Seeing the way her lips pressed together and the narrowing of her eyes, he guessed she was. "However, if you're planning to walk, I'd say it'd take a day or two. Or more." He didn't add all the factors to consider. How fast they could walk. How much luggage they insisted on carrying. The lack of food and water. He'd let her figure it out on her own. "They'll send out someone to investigate when they realize the stagecoach isn't coming. Probably a couple of men. Might be someone here tomorrow."

She scrubbed her lips together. A sign she was thinking, if he recalled correctly. He'd not forgotten one tiny detail of her mannerisms, though heaven knows he'd tried.

"Auntie, what are we going to do?" Rosie half sobbed the words.

"We'll figure out something." Mae looked at Austin as she spoke.

He felt her words clear down to his toes and knew she expected him to offer a solution. But what could he do? He looked up the bank. Didn't fancy trying to get them up there. He ran his gaze along the embankment. The slope appeared gentler down the way.

"We could climb up there." He pointed.

"Then what?"

"I'll escort you to Logan Crossing. We could take turns riding and walking."

"What about my things?" She nodded toward the crate of books and lifted her gaze to the top of the hill where he'd seen clothing scattered about.

"Would you prefer to stay here and wait for me to ride back to the fort and get a wagon?"

She considered the offer. Then shook her head. "Those men might come back." She went to the crate and tried to move it.

"Are you planning to carry that?"

"Of course not. But I might put it in the coach so it isn't left behind."

"Just leave it. You can come back and get it."

She straightened. "I guess I don't have any choice. Come on, children." With the pair in her wake, she headed the direction Austin had indicated.

He followed them. She was as headstrong as he remembered without the countering balance of the sweetness he'd known. Of course, that lack might be because of their past.

OF ALL THE men in all the big wide west, why did the man who came to her rescue have to be Austin Wagoner? Mae held back an audible groan, not wanting to draw the children's attention to her.

Austin had ridden from her life five years ago without so much as a 'see you later' or, if that wasn't in his plans, not even 'goodbye.' A word of explanation might have been nice. Made the parting a little easier to endure. Especially when he'd asked her to marry him only a few days prior. Said he wanted to ask permission from her brother first, he being her guardian and all. Said he meant to do it the right way. He'd given her the locket she always kept with her. She no longer wore it around her neck. She didn't need or want the constant memory of what they'd once had. It was in her luggage which, according to Austin, was up the hill.

She'd never be able to forgive him for riding from her life. Leaving her alone, nursing a broken heart while dealing with her brother's death. Shot he was. Part of a bank robbery. The sheriff didn't know whose bullet had claimed Colin's life, which was both mercy and torture. A part of her wanted to track down the shooter and demand justice, even though she understood Colin was in the wrong and his sins had cost him his life.

Knowing the facts didn't stop her heart from wanting revenge, though she would never admit that's what it was. She simply needed to confront the man who'd shot her brother and make him say he was sorry. Again, she dismissed the knowledge that Colin had been shot running from the law after he'd been part of a bank robbery.

Now, just when she'd turned another page in her life, hoping to find a place where she and the children could belong, Austin rode into her life, flooding her mind with sweet memories heavily tinged with anger and sorrow.

The sooner she got to where she was going, the sooner she could begin afresh. And finally, forget Austin. Those thoughts drove her to a furious pace until she reached the spot where they were meant to climb. She studied it. It was steeper than she expected.

Austin edged past her and led the way. Colin scrambled onward, clutching at the bushes to keep from sliding. Rosie followed her brother, slipping often. Austin grabbed her hand and pulled her upward until she reached the top.

Mae gritted her teeth and began the ascent. She would do this on her own. If two children needed minimal help, she needed none. Her feet slid and she landed on her knees, grabbing at bushes to stop herself from slipping further.

Austin edged down to her. "Give me your hand."

No. She would not. She reached for bushes higher up the slope, managed to pull herself upward.

Austin stayed just ahead, holding out a hand.

She continued without accepting his offer.

They were almost at the top and suddenly there were no more bushes. She leaned forward, her hands to the shaley ground at her nose. Nothing about her position felt stable. An apt description of her entire life, she thought with a degree of irritation mixed with a pinch of humor.

Austin's hand closed around one of hers and her world spun wildly as he pulled her upward.

She collapsed at the top of the incline, her heart pounding like a dozen racing horses. Only because of the climb, she firmly insisted. It had absolutely nothing to do with the shock of remembrance triggered by Austin's touch. Her thoughts absolutely had *not* conjured up scene after scene of them holding hands and running through a field of flowers, or walking hand in hand along a dusty road with nothing in mind but enjoying each other's company. And she certainly had not thought of a moonlit evening when she'd seen stars in her eyes as he held her hands to his chest and confessed his love.

Love was but a word to him.

Her heart and thoughts back to normal, she jumped to her feet. "Come along, children." She headed down the road to where the stagecoach had been stopped.

Ten steps later, she drew to a halt. The others stopped and looked at her.

"What's wrong, Auntie?" Colin asked, bouncing from foot to foot. Always eager to rush into things.

"Colin, wait here with Rosie. I need to talk to Austin." Though by rights, they should address him as Mr. Wagoner. She'd remember that next time. "May we have a word?" She went a distance from the children, grateful that he followed without question. Dropping her voice to a whisper, she said, "The driver and shotgun rider?"

"Dead."

"I thought so. I don't want the children to see them." She glanced around, hoping against hope that there was another route. But the road ran north and south. She assumed the direction from seeing the mountains and knowing that was west. There were trees to one side of the trail and the drop-off to the other. They'd have to pass the bodies. Besides, she wanted to gather up her belongings.

"Stay here with them and let me take care of it. Keep the children occupied looking the other direction." He jogged away.

She rejoined her niece and nephew. "Look how far we've come." She pointed behind them and they turned. "It's hard to think that this morning we were in Fort Macleod. Colin, remember how excited you were to see the Mounties?" She'd been a bit awed too. They were so regal in their red serge.

Colin grew serious. "I think I want to be a Mountie when I grow up."

"That would be nice." Better to be on the right side of the law. She'd never told the children the truth about how their father died. And didn't plan to ever do so.

Rosie grew dreamy-eyed. "Maybe I'll marry a Mountie."

Mae chuckled. "Seems Colin wasn't the only one who admired them." She badly wanted to glance over her shoulder to see what Austin was doing but didn't want to take the chance of having the children look in that direction.

"Maybe we should go back there," Rosie said. "The Mounties would help us."

"I'm sure they would, but first we'd have to get there. But maybe it's better to head to our destination. I'm anxious to see the new schoolhouse where I'll teach and the attached living quarters." The description that the Arbuckles had provided made it sound appealing. Six young families living nearby. Five school-aged children. Seven with the two she had with her. A nice small class. She'd be able to devote lots of attention to each child. No one would be able to accuse her of favoring her own niece and nephew. Not that she ever had, but it didn't stop others from thinking she did. And providing them a reason to not renew her contract.

She was tired of moving from place to place. The children needed stability. She hoped to get that at the Circle A Ranch.

Hopefully, this present situation wasn't a harbinger of things to come.

Rosie was busy telling Colin about the young Mountie who had carried her over a mud puddle. It had made quite an impression. Mae knew the girl missed her father and mother. She'd done her best to be a mother figure for them, but both children hungered after a father figure. She hoped that her new position would introduce good men into their lives. Mrs. Arbuckle had told about raising six boys who were now married and lived nearby. The way she spoke of them informed Mae that the men were of noble character. Just what Rosie and Colin needed.

Footsteps coming toward her alerted her that Austin was coming back.

She slowly turned, reluctant to look at him. She told herself he'd changed. His hair was still brown. His brown eyes were no longer warm and welcoming, but his gaze guarded and distant. He'd filled out some. He'd be… she pretended to think about it…twenty-eight now and had a mature look about him. He had the look of a man who had seen more of life than he cared for.

She stopped her thoughts right there. At one time she might have guessed, even known, things about him that weren't said, but five years meant a lot of changes.

He nodded and she understood he'd moved the bodies. She didn't ask how or where.

"Come, children. Let's see to our belongings."

The four of them marched down the road.

"My shirt." Colin ran ahead, picked up his shirt and gave it a shake. "Good as new," he announced.

Rosie let out a squeak. "My clothes are all over the ground."

"Pick them up and put them in your valise—" which lay upside down nearby "—everything will wash."

She swallowed a groan at the way her clothing was

scattered about. Some things had been trampled on. Rather than complain, she retrieved her satchel, shook each item, folded it carefully, and returned each to the traveling bag. And if tears stung the backs of her eyes, she wasn't about to admit it. Or heaven forbid, reveal it.

Thankfully, Austin had gone to get his horses. By the time he rejoined them, Mae had her own bag packed and had assisted the children. Had he purposely left them alone to do this? Perhaps not wanting to intrude on their efforts. If so, was it out of concern and kindness or a wish to avoid witnessing their emotions?

There was a time she might have known, but he was now a stranger. Perhaps he'd always been one.

She stood by the children as Austin faced them. He'd removed his gun belt. She couldn't think what it meant nor how she felt about it. If those four robbers were still around, a man wearing a gun might be a good thing. However, she didn't want the children to be upset by the idea of Austin needing to wear one. She decided she was grateful he'd put it away.

"I'll tie your bags to the pack saddle," he said, reaching for Colin's satchel. One by one, he secured their bags, then looked at Mae. "Are you ready to go?"

"I certainly am."

"Then you and Rosie can ride. Colin can perch on the pack saddle."

"And you?"

"I'll walk for now." He lifted Colin to the back of the packhorse as he talked, then went to the side of his riding horse. "This is Benton. He's a good horse. Lots of heart." He gave Mae an expectant look.

It hit her that he was waiting for her to get on the back of the horse.

"Mae, I recall you ride."

"Sidesaddle. And with a riding skirt." The skirt she wore was much too slim to allow her to be modest riding astride. Her cheeks burned to think about it.

He studied her then nodded and went to the packs and removed a blanket. "You can cover your legs with this."

She wanted to argue, refuse, but either she walked all the way or rode part-time. She was used to walking, but not the kind of distances that lay ahead. Besides, she was still a little shaky from falling down the hill. There was no point in wasting time. Drawing in a steadying breath, she joined Austin at the side of his horse and placed one foot in his cupped hands. As she swung to the back of the horse, her skirt rode upward.

"Turn away." She settled herself in the saddle, spread the blanket across her legs then said, "I'm decent." *Lord God, don't let anyone from the Circle A Ranch see me.* They'd surely deem her behavior inappropriate for a teacher. She didn't want to lose this job before she even started it.

Austin lifted Rosie up behind Mae, took the reins of Colin's horse and started down the trail. Her horse —Benton—followed along without any guidance from her.

With Austin's back to her and Rosie pressed to her back, Mae took in a long, satisfying breath. She supposed if she needed rescuing—or only just a little assistance—she could do worse than to have her rescuer be someone she knew.

They plodded along with nothing but the thud of horse hooves, the songs of nearby birds, and, in the distance, the roll of thunder.

Thunder?

She looked to the sky. To the west, clouds twisted and rolled over the mountains. Black and threatening.

She glanced back to Austin. Had he noticed? Was he concerned?

He gazed toward the west. His profile revealed a downturned mouth and a firmly set jaw. He looked back at her. "Storm coming. We're going to get soaked unless we shelter somewhere."

A soaking would make them all miserable and put the children in danger of getting sick. Shelter sounded good, but Mae studied their surroundings. There was nothing but trees with no leaves. A few evergreen trees, but as far as she could tell, nothing that offered shelter.

She shivered.

First, the robbery and crash. Then having Austin ride into their lives. Now a storm.

And she had no choice but to accept his help to get her out of this situation.

Things were definitely going from bad to worse.

She prayed fervently it wasn't the beginning of a downward spiral.

Hadn't she had enough of that in the past?

2

Austin might have pushed on, enduring the rain. But he didn't think the others were up to the misery of a cold soaking.

"If you agree," he addressed Mae, "we'll stop here and wait out the storm." The clouds approached quickly, so they'd have to hurry.

She looked around. "Seems to me we might as well ride as stand in the trees with no shelter."

"I can make a shelter." Taking her agreement for granted, he led the packhorse to the trees and lifted Colin down. He set Rosie on the ground and then studied the situation with Mae for a moment, but there wasn't time to fuss about the best way to do things. He lifted her from the saddle and put her on her feet, ignoring her sputtered protests. Moving with urgency and the skill of having done this a few times, he looked around for a suitable location. As if an answer to an unspoken prayer, he immediately saw a tangle of fallen trees. Perfect. He led the horses to the trees, unpacked them and set to work.

"Colin, Rosie, see what you can find for wood to burn." Hopefully it would keep them busy so they didn't have time to stand there rocking back and forth in worry as they watched him.

They scurried about, bringing in fallen branches as he stretched his tarp over the fallen limbs he'd chosen and secured it in front, leaving a small opening for a doorway. The wind would blow away from the door, making it possible to have a fire and to stay dry… at least until the rain came and drowned the flames. Finished, he stood back to look at his shelter. It was small for four of them, but would have to do.

"Crawl inside." The children went first. He turned to Mae. "You're next."

Mae hurried inside to join Colin and Rosie.

Good. They would be safe and dry. He pushed in as much wood as he could and started the fire in front of the opening. He'd keep it going as long as he could. But eventually, the rain would quench it. He moved the saddle packs close and then squeezed himself into the little corner left.

He tried not to touch Mae, which was easier said than done. The shelter would have been adequate for one person. It was tight as a drum with four of them there. He stretched his legs out the opening, keeping them to one side to avoid the fire.

"You hit me," Colin said.

"Can't help it. I've got no room." Rosie sounded fretful.

"Children, we're all crowded. But we'll be dry." Mae spoke gently.

Austin pulled one saddlebag closer and untied the flaps. "Anyone hungry?" he asked, pulling out a sack of crackers and biscuits. He passed it to Mae. "Help yourself."

She was hunched at his elbow, her attention on the children, allowing him time to study her without her being aware of it. Every feature was so familiar. Even the tiny scar on her chin that she'd told him she'd gotten when she tripped and fell on the frozen ground when she was a child.

Familiar and yet now a stranger. He felt like he dangled between the past and the present. With nothing in sight for his future but another winter in his cabin. Staying alive kept him busy. Finding and preparing food. Gathering wood. Melting snow for water. That and his carving.

She handed the sack of food back to him and met his stare.

He hadn't meant for her to catch him studying her, but couldn't force himself to turn away. Feelings burned inside him. Raw, painful, regretful. Determination had gotten him through the last five years, but it picked this time and place to abandon him. Instead, yearning and remembrances surfaced with a force that robbed him of reason.

"Here. We have some and thank you." Mae shook the sack to indicate he should take it.

His hand moved of its own accord. His gaze followed the movement of his arm. He glued his attention to the sack that was now in his possession.

Words balanced on the tip of his tongue. Things he wanted to say to her. Had wanted to say five years ago and every day since. But the same reasons for holding them back existed now even as they had then. There was no apology big enough, no word powerful enough to undo the fact that he'd shot her brother.

To be here with him must be a worse shock than the robbery and crash.

Why him? That thought had been his constant companion since he'd rescued them. Though he did not yet have them to safety.

But he'd do everything in his power to get them there. *Heavenly Father, You have helped me to survive these past five years. I beg of You to see me through the next few days. Please.*

Rain drops pattered on their shelter. Wind tugged at the canvas, bringing with it a drop in temperature.

"For goodness' sake," Mae said with some passion. "Get inside before you're soaked."

"I'll crowd you."

"I'd say it can't be helped."

She was more than generous to allow him to be so close, considering what he'd done and what she must surely think of him. But then she'd always been kind and generous. He drew in his legs. They sat shoulder to shoulder. He pulled his knees to his chest, trying to make himself as small as possible. Being a tall man was mighty inconvenient at the moment.

The children turned so they could look at the adults.

Austin could face down a man of any size, but it was all he could do not to squirm before the intensity of their study.

"What'd you do with your gun?" Colin asked.

"Colin," Mae scolded.

"I'm just asking a question."

"It's all right. I put it away. Don't figure I'll need it." Maybe this time it would be for good.

"You shoot people?"

"Colin!"

Poor Mae, having the facts out there so plain and unavoidable.

"Not if I don't have to."

"Why would you have to?"

It seemed the children had been spared the facts about their father's death. That provided Austin a pinch of comfort.

"Like, if somebody asks too many questions?" Rosie jabbed her brother.

Austin laughed. "That's not reason enough."

"What is?" Colin seemed set on having an answer.

"Well, let's say someone held a gun on your aunt and threatened to hurt her. I might think that's a reason to shoot him."

Mae's indrawn breath sucked the air from their tiny shelter.

Austin might have tried to explain himself, tell her it was just an example. He wouldn't tell her that he would face any enemy to defend her. Even himself. But at that moment, the rain pounded overhead with such force that it drowned out conversation.

The fire sputtered, sizzled, and died. There would be no more heat. Thankfully they all wore warm coats. He'd tossed in the blanket and now pulled it toward Mae. "Wrap up and keep warm." He spoke close enough to her ear for her to hear. And close enough he breathed in the scent of her. Lavender. Still using the same soap.

She tucked the blanket around the children and wrapped her arms around herself.

His body blocked the entrance, also preventing some of the cold air from entering. Despite his warm coat, the far side of him was cold. The near side, next to Mae, was toasty. It was all he could do not to lean closer, sharing as much body heat as he could.

She shifted. Her shoulder blocking any idea that there might exist a possibility of being welcome. They were in this out of necessity and she was polite enough to make the best of it.

The rain settled into a steady pounding, making it possible to hear each other though Austin didn't think there was much to be said between himself and Mae.

Colin let out a long sigh. "How long we gonna be here?"

"Until the rain stops," Mae said.

"Unless you want to go out in the rain and get all wet." Rosie turned to Mae. "It might be one way of getting him bathed."

Colin huffed.

Austin couldn't contain a snicker. He wondered if his amusement would offend Mae, but she showed no reaction.

"Rosie, honey, I think we'll wait until he can get into a warm water bath."

Colin turned eager eyes to Austin. "I seen how you wore your gun. You a real gunman?"

"Colin, it's I saw and it's also impolite to ask personal questions," Mae said.

Austin wanted to erase any idealism the boy might have about guns. "I'm really a mountain man. I have a cabin west of here. Up in the mountains. Prettiest spot you ever saw. It's by a lake. In the winter the snow gets pretty deep and sometimes I have to shovel a lot to get to my woodshed. But in the summer there are wild alpine flowers everywhere. The water is as blue as anything you could imagine."

Rosie lay on her stomach, her chin propped on her hands. "Who do you live with?"

"Well, let's see." He pretended to give it some thought. "There are three crows that hang around and make a nuisance of themselves. They wait for me to throw out some scraps and then they fight over them."

"But what about—"

He held up a hand to stop her question. "Then there's a chipmunk who steals from the crows and scampers away making a chip-chip sound. He's a real rascal." Seeing Rosie's protest about to explode from her, he rushed on. "A skunk visits every spring. Leaves her babies under the wood pile. You ever seen a baby skunk?" The children shook their heads.

Mae turned toward him, watching him talk.

"Baby skunks are very cute. And funny to watch. You know what the trouble with them is?" Three heads shook no.

"They grow up to be adult skunks and…" He held his nose and made a face.

The children laughed.

He was almost certain Mae smiled. He was so distracted that Rosie got her question out.

"Do other people live with you?"

"Not real people."

Rosie and Colin both stared opened mouth.

It was Mae who voiced the question. "You have imaginary friends?" Her shock and disbelief were as plain as the dampness shrouding them.

He laughed, genuinely enjoying her reaction. "They're very real. Just not alive."

"You live with dead people?" She blinked and tried to edge away from him but she had no place to go.

"Relax." He couldn't keep the amusement from his voice. "They're wooden people."

"What does that mean?" She tossed an incredulous look over her shoulder.

"I carve figures. Some are small enough to sit on a shelf. Some are bigger, almost life-size." He wouldn't inform her that he'd made one that looked almost like her. It was lifeless, wooden, speechless but it was the most he could ever expect.

"Well, that's a relief. For a minute I wondered if we were in the hands of a crazy man."

"What would you have done if you thought I was?"

"I'd figure out something." Her gaze held his in a warning and, perhaps, challenge.

He nodded. "I recall a similar conversation a few years back when a young lady informed an overly bold man who was bothering her friend that she would use the poker from the fireplace to brand him and then drive him from the place."

She blinked and turned her head away from him,

but he knew she remembered saying those words. Did she also remember how he'd hugged her and said he was proud of her? And how he'd said she should never be afraid to defend herself or those she loved.

He shifted a bit, focusing on the storm outside their little shelter. Those same strengths that he admired and praised were the very reason he knew she would never forgive him. Hadn't she once said exactly that? He recalled her words as clearly as if she uttered them this very minute. They had echoed persistently through his head since he'd ridden out of her life.

If anyone hurts someone I care about I would never forgive them. Nor would I let them know a moment's peace until they'd paid for what they did.

Now that she had the opportunity, would she find a way to make him pay, or had five years been long enough for her anger to abate?

A sharp sound like a gunshot shattered the silence.

Was there someone out there?

He jerked toward the door.

Mae strained at his shoulder. "What was that?"

"I don't know." He listened for any telltale sound.

MAE COULD ALMOST WELCOME the explosive sound that served to distract her from racing down memory lane at the words Austin spoke. She recalled the incident he mentioned. Just as clearly as she remembered the feel of his arms around her as he said he approved of her brave stand.

She still felt that way, although five years had eased her anger. Now she would probably only use her words. Let the person know how much her brother's death had affected them all.

He eased back when no other sound came. "I suppose it was a tree snapping in the wind."

She gladly accepted his suggestion. Reason told her that the robbers would have no reason to return. They'd taken everything they deemed of value. By now, they would be miles away.

The children stirred. She understood how uncomfortable they must be pressed together in this tiny shelter. But at least they were dry and hopefully warm. The damp air was chilly, clawing at her bones.

Mae's discomfort had less to do with being crowded than it did with having her thoughts pressing at her. To have Austin at her side, his arm warm and protective, his body blocking the cold and rain, was a dream come true. Every cell in her body carried an emptiness that could be filled by nothing and no one but this man. She'd learned to live with that hollow feeling.

Five-year-old questions battered at the inside of her head. What had she done that was so awful he'd ridden away without a word? Had he discovered some dreadful secret about her? Or had he simply grown tired of her?

She pressed her lips tight and focused on the children. They were all that mattered now.

Rosie stared at Austin.

Mae wondered what was going through the girl's head. She was quieter, more thoughtful than her younger brother. Not that she seemed to remember much about her parents. They'd both been so young. Colin had been three, Rosie five. Rosie had vague memories of her mother but at least she didn't remember the bad things.

"Mr. Wagoner, how long have you lived with your wooden friends?" Rosie said

The way Austin jerked, Mae guessed his thoughts had been far away. What she wouldn't give to be privy to them.

"This will be my third winter in my cabin, enjoying my quiet associates." He chuckled at his little joke.

Two years unaccounted for. If they were alone she might have asked where he was and what he did those years. But it wasn't a discussion she wanted to have with two children listening.

"Well, it sounds lonely." Rosie's tone informed them that she found the idea unacceptable. "I'd sooner have Colin for company than no one."

Austin laughed. "You're fortunate to have a brother."

"Guess so. Do you have a brother or sister?"

"I once had a brother. But he's dead."

Mae admired him for speaking so calmly. "I remember you telling me about him." Beecher had been older. A hero in Austin's eyes. Beecher was good with a gun and taught Austin to be as well. But Beecher had run into someone even faster. Austin had said it drove him to practice more and more. He got so good, he got hired by a sheriff. He'd told Mae he meant to stay on the right side of the law. She'd wondered a time or two if learning that Colin, Senior was a bank robber had somehow influenced Austin's opinion of her.

"That's sad," Rosie said.

"My mama and papa are dead." Colin got that awed tone he always got when he spoke of his parents.

Mae could never quite understand if it meant he felt he was in a different class because of the fact or if he was voicing an emptiness within – though she rather suspected it was a bit of both.

"I'm sorry." Austin's voice was soft.

"But we got Aunt Mae." Colin gave her a wide, sweet smile. "She's a good aunt. And a good teacher. Even if people say otherwise."

"Honey, they don't say I'm not a good teacher."

"Silly," Rosie added. "They just say she can't teach other children if we're there."

She felt Austin looking at her but kept her gaze on the children. The pressure of his arm against hers, the familiar sound of his voice, and the ache of missing him would be her undoing if she wasn't careful.

"Is that right?" he asked.

"Some parents objected." She didn't plan to say more. The accusations had been unfounded. "I never gave either of the children preferential treatment." So much for not saying anything more, but the unfairness of it burned at her insides.

Austin exerted just enough pressure on her shoulder that she knew he intentionally did it. "I'm sure you didn't. Your sense of justice is far too strong."

Completely forgetting that she meant to avoid looking at him, she jerked around. He was so close she could see the way squint lines fanned out from the corners of his eyes. He must have shaved this morning, for there was barely a shadow of whiskers. She pressed the tip of her tongue to her upper lip and breathed slowly as a rush of emotions almost drowned her.

She'd loved this man with such purity and conviction. Even his failure had not quenched that love. But she must not let her feelings escape from the cage to which she had relegated them.

He smiled gently. Lifted a hand as if to touch her. Seemed to think better of it and lowered it again.

Swallowing hard, sure everyone could hear her, she jerked her gaze away to stare at the canvas protecting them. Water spots were visible. It wouldn't be long before there were drips.

Could they get any more miserable?

She might have asked too soon because lightning flashed and thunder rolled. She jerked. It sounded very close.

Rosie was afraid of such storms and whimpered.

Mae would have pulled her to her lap, but there simply wasn't room and she settled for patting Rosie's back. "We're all right."

At that moment, a flash lit up the shelter, momentarily blinding her and a clap of thunder followed almost instantly.

"That was close," Colin said, sounding suitably impressed.

Austin leaned to look out the opening. "You have to see this."

At the tone of his voice, Mae and the children edged forward. Colin peered out under Austin's arm. Rosie squeezed in over the top of her brother. That left Mae no choice but to look over Austin's shoulder. Her chin touched the fabric of his coat. She inhaled the scent of smoke, rain, and leather. Her insides jittered in a frenzied dance of longing and regrets, but at what she saw, she forgot everything but the scene before her.

3

Austin watched the tree burn like a large torch.

"What happened?" Colin asked.

"It was struck by lightning."

Rosie shivered, the movement racing along his arm. "Are we going to get hit?" Fear thinned her words.

"It's not likely. Lightning goes for the tallest object."

"So if we were standing out there, you'd be hit?" Colin sounded intrigued by the idea. "Cause you're the tallest."

Austin chuckled. "Pretty sure the trees are taller."

"Yeah, I guess so."

Austin turned a couple of degrees. He told himself it was so he could look at Mae, but with her head touching his shoulder the movement only served to allow him to press his cheek to her hair. "I can't tell if he's disappointed or relieved," he murmured.

Mae drew back. He expected nothing else. Then she leaned closer to watch the fire. They were all mesmerized by the sight.

"Will it spread?" She spoke so softly, he guessed she hoped the children wouldn't hear.

"I don't think so. It's pretty wet out there." Though the rain had quit, water dripped from every branch.

He was almost sorry to realize the storm was almost over. They'd be able to leave this little shelter where necessity had crowded them together. He knew he couldn't expect her to allow such closeness once they resumed their journey.

"We'll soon be able to move on." Her tone informed him that the time to leave couldn't come soon enough to suit her.

For a few minutes conversation ended as they watched the tree burn. When it was nothing more than a glowing red stack, Austin moved.

"Let's eat some lunch before we think about leaving." He handed around hunks of cheese and jerky from his supplies.

"This how you eat at your house?" Colin asked.

"It's a cabin," Rosie corrected.

"I eat better than this. I bake biscuits. Even bread."

"You do?" Rosie was suitably impressed. "What else?"

"I like cookies, so I've learned to make them. Molasses cookies are my favorite."

Both children's eyes had grown wide in disbelief. Or was it awe?

"I have a little garden." Though most of his efforts would be wasted this year, seeing as he'd spent the bulk of his summer at the Big Sky Ranch dealing with rustlers. Thankfully, he hadn't had to shoot any of them. Seems his reputation was enough to thwart any challenge. And then the Mounties had taken over. "If I get back in time I'll dig potatoes, carrots, and turnips and store them for the winter."

Colin and Rosie nodded, wanting more.

"I hunt for my meat. I actually eat pretty good."

"You don't have to drink milk." Colin made it sound like that was a bonus.

"I would like to have milk and cream, but I don't have a cow."

"How big is this cabin of yours?" Mae's question surprised him. He didn't think she would join the conversation.

"It's plenty big enough for me and my fellow dwellers."

The children giggled at the mention of his friends.

He looked at Mae as he spoke. "I have a good stove, a table large enough for eating and working at. I have a comfortable chair. That's where I read—"

"What do you read?"

He wondered at this sudden interest but welcomed it. "I get books and newspapers when I come out for supplies. I have my Bible which provides hours of reading." Did she recall the times they had sat beneath a leafy tree and read the Word together? "Plus, I have several old favorites."

"Aunt Mae makes me read out loud." Colin's voice was so mournful that Austin knew the boy didn't care for reading.

"I expect there will come a time that you'll enjoy reading so much that you'll be grateful to your aunt. When that time comes be sure you remember to thank her."

Colin didn't answer.

Rosie patted his back. "Never mind. You're good at other things."

"No, I'm not."

Rosie didn't give either adult a chance to argue the point. "You run fast. You can throw a ball a far distance. You bring in wood for Auntie. And you're kind."

"I am?"

"Most of the time."

Impressed by Rosie's words, Austin glanced to Mae.

She beamed at the children. "Rosie, that was very kind of you. And you're right. Colin, you are good at many things."

Austin leaned closer, though there was little enough distance separating them. "I can see you've done a good job, Auntie."

She darted a glance at him then jerked away, but he'd seen enough to know his words had surprised her and at the same time pleased her.

There was no sign or mention of a man in her life. "It must be hard raising them on your own."

Her gaze didn't falter.

He waited to see if she would correct his assumption and when she didn't, his breath whistled through his teeth. Not that it mattered. He wouldn't be filling that position. In order to corral any thought headed in that direction, he turned to study the outdoors. "I'll go see to the horses. The rest of you stay here until I say. The grass is dripping. No point in getting wet any sooner than we have to."

The horses were huddled under the trees. At least they hadn't been struck by lightning. He was amazed they hadn't broken free when the tree burst into flames.

"Benton, old boy. You're a mighty good horse." He figured Benton's calmness kept the packhorse from bolting. He carried an old blanket in his supplies and used it to rub the animals down. By the time he finished, the sun was out and he left them to dry in the sunshine while he repacked their things.

"Are you going to roll up the canvas while it's still wet?" Mae asked as he began to fold it.

"I'll hang it to dry as soon as we get somewhere."

"Might be mildewed by then."

He stared at her, surprise making his words intense. "Are you suggesting we stay here until it's dry?"

She blinked and then chuckled. "Just being a school marm and pointing out the consequences." She drew in a breath that made her shoulders rise and fall. "As if you don't know already."

He wasn't sure she was talking about the wet tarp or something else entirely. "I'm thinking it's more important to get the three of you to your destination. Or at least to adequate shelter."

"Of course. Though that served the purpose." She tipped her head to the bunch of branches that had formed the skeleton for holding the tarpaulin.

Austin focused his attention on the canvas. Was she saying that she hadn't minded being crowded up with him? Might even have enjoyed it?

Nah. She must mean something else entirely. His brain was so muddled he couldn't think what.

He secured the folded tarp to the packs and tacked up the horses. Colin and Rosie had gone to have a closer look at the tree that still glowed like hot coals. "Everyone ready to go?" he called.

They scampered back.

He lifted Colin to the back of the packhorse. Rosie waited at Benton's back. Austin turned to help Mae. She shook her head.

"I'll walk."

"Walk? There's no need. You can ride." He sounded as confused as he felt.

"I don't mind stretching my legs for a bit."

"Oh." Not that it had crossed his mind that she wanted to keep him company. He lifted Rosie to Benton's back, took up the reins and led the horses down the muddy trail, Mae at his side. "I remember you used to like walking." Probably not the wisest thing to say.

"I still do, though it's not always convenient. The children don't always want to accompany me and I can't leave them alone."

"That's hard."

She held up a hand. "Don't get me wrong. I don't mind any little inconvenience that comes with raising them. To be able to do so is a special privilege and pleasure."

There wasn't much he could say to that. "I was surprised to hear their mother had died."

"She never recovered from losing her husband. I suppose you could say she died of a broken heart, or at least that's what people liked to say."

"You don't agree?"

"I won't speak ill of the dead, but I would think her two children were enough reason to keep living."

Guilt and regret seared his insides. So he was to blame for her death as well. It was a wonder Mae didn't find something and beat his brains out. He narrowed his eyes and studied her without turning his head. Was she simply waiting until she had a suitable weapon? Had she learned to shoot a gun? He'd not seen any evidence of one when her things were scattered on the ground. Nor had he had a glimpse of anything gun-like strapped to her leg when she rode. Yes, he admitted it. He'd stolen a glance.

"I'm curious," she said. "You said you've spent two —or was it three—years in your cabin. What did you do the other years?" She kept her gaze straight ahead, but her voice revealed more than idle curiosity.

He wondered what she really wanted to know. Had she tried to track him down and wanted to know where she'd failed? "I worked for a cattle company or two. Went down to Texas."

"What's in Texas?" Again a bland tone that carried a hint of something else.

"Lots of cattle." And cattle rustlers. And lawmen and ranchers in need of a fast gun to uphold the law, but he wasn't about to tell her that. "Lots of cowboys. And bluebonnets."

That got her attention. She stopped in the middle of the road and turned to face him.

"Your eyes are the same color." He hadn't meant to say that. But there was no putting the words back in his mouth where they should have stayed. "Sorry. I have no right."

She started walking again without any response. Then she stopped. "I believe I'll ride for a while."

The message was as clear as if written in large black letters across the sky.

He'd offended her and she didn't want to walk with him anymore.

"I'm sorry," he said again.

For an answer, she went to the horse. "Help me up."

He cupped his hands so she could step up. He held the blanket out to her and averted his eyes as she covered her legs. He'd offended her enough already without letting her see him looking at her.

She settled in the saddle, Rosie clinging to her back. "Thank you." Mae didn't even look at him as she spoke.

He handed her the reins and went to lead the packhorse. He'd spoken out of turn, ignored how she must feel about him. He'd gotten exactly what he deserved.

Knowing so did not make it any easier to accept.

Mae sucked in slow deep breaths. She was an expert at calming herself. Or at least she should be. She'd had plenty of practice over the years. Dealing with one death after another... alone. Facing her sense of abandonment. Being dismissed time and again for no justifiable reason. She put the criticism against her down to jealousy. But no matter how slow and deep she breathed, her insides remained in turmoil.

Why Austin? Yes, she'd prayed for rescue. But why Austin? And why did he have to speak of the past? Mentioning his Bible reading. Taking her right back. Sitting under a tree, overlooking the river and watching the boats pass by had been one of the things she had enjoyed doing with him. They had started a little practice of bringing along a Bible. She'd read to him. Or he'd read to her. They'd talk about what the passage meant. They even had favorite verses. Did he remember that?

She still had the Bible they'd used. Like the heart-shaped locket, she'd kept it even though the memories that it triggered were painful.

Then he had to go and make a comment about her eyes. Blueberry eyes he used to call them. But bluebonnet eyes sounded even better.

But she did not want him to say anything about her eyes or remind her of anything in the past. The past was gone. Never to be remembered if she could achieve her goal. What lay ahead was all that mattered.

"I wonder when we'll get to the Circle A Ranch," Rosie said.

Mae heard the weariness and worry in the girl's voice. Understood that life had held too many uncertainties for Rosie to feel safe and settled. She pushed aside her own thoughts and answered her.

"I don't know, but I know one thing for certain."

"What?"

"God is with us right this moment. Remember the verses we learned in Psalm one hundred and thirty-nine?" She waited, hoping one of the children would recite the verses.

"I remember some," Colin said. "There is not a word in my tongue, but, the Lord knows it."

The words were imperfectly quoted, but Colin had certainly retained the meaning. "Very good, Colin," she said. "I'm surprised that's the verse you remember."

"Auntie, if God knows what we're going to say, why doesn't He stop us from saying bad things?"

This wasn't the direction she'd planned to take when she brought up the chapter, but it was obviously something that concerned Colin and needed to be addressed.

"Colin, God allows us to make our own choices. But He will certainly help us if we ask."

He lifted his face toward the sky. "God, help me not to say bad things."

Mae smiled at how literal Colin was. She returned her gaze to the trail ahead. But her eyes stopped at Austin. He glanced over his shoulder and grinned at her. No doubt he'd heard every word. Well, it couldn't be helped and besides, she didn't care. He'd assist her to a safe place, for which she was grateful, and then he'd ride away again.

Shifting her gaze away and bringing her thoughts back to her conversation with Rosie, she asked, "Rosie, what do you remember about the Psalm we learned?"

In a voice as sweet as an angel's, Rosie recited, "'If I take the wings of the morning, and dwell in the uttermost parts of the sea; even there shall thy hand lead me, and thy right hand shall hold me.'" The girl's voice filled with awe. "That means God is leading us and holding us, doesn't it?"

"That's exactly what it means."

"Then I guess we're safe."

"We certainly are." The verses were the reminder she needed. God would never leave them. He would guide their steps. She had nothing to fear. Except maybe her memories.

She must confront those wayward thoughts. She reined in, drawing Austin's attention.

"Is there something wrong?" he asked.

"I believe I'll walk for a bit." She struggled to get off the horse as her leg got entangled with the blanket. Before she could straighten herself out Austin lifted her down.

His hands on her waist sent butterfly wings

dancing along her nerves. She murmured thanks and quickly stepped away from him.

He rubbed his hands along his legs as if trying to remove her from his palms.

The butterfly wings turned to wasp stings…a pain as familiar as her own breath. Needing a moment to compose herself, she helped Rosie into the saddle and patted her leg. Seeing the peace in her niece's face, she filled her lungs with courage and went ahead of the horse.

Austin took up the reins and walked at her side. "It's nice that you teach the children to memorize Bible verses."

"I am a teacher after all." Her snippy response likely suggested she was a cranky one, but she couldn't help it. Her raw memories were getting the best of her.

No, she would not allow that. If the past five years had taught her anything, it was that she could handle any situation. With God's help.

She put the width of the road between them. To divert herself, she studied her surroundings. The deciduous trees were leafless, except for a few stubborn, yellowed leaves that clung tobare branches. It seemed a fitting portrayal of her life. The death of her brother and sister-in-law, and the abandonment of the man she thought loved her, had sucked the color from her life. But she would not let it destroy her. If only because she had two children who needed her and whom she loved dearly. And because she was too stubborn to let those things defeat her.

"I have enjoyed seeing the mountains," she said by way of averting any probing questions.

"'God is our refuge and strength, a very present help in trouble. Therefore will not we fear, though the earth be removed, and though the mountains be carried into the midst of the sea'"

Despite her resolve to avoid looking at him, her gaze jerked his direction.

"That's from the Psalms." He looked straight ahead, not meeting her gaze.

Psalm forty-six. She knew it well. It was a Psalm she and Austin had read together and promised they would never forget the last verses. 'Be still, and know that I am God: I will be exalted among the heathen, I will be exalted in the earth. The Lord of hosts is with us; the God of Jacob is our refuge.' At the time, they had talked about how bad things should drive them to God, not be allowed to form a wedge between them.

"I remember," she said, expecting he would take it to mean she knew what Psalm he meant.

"You said the death of your parents made you question God's hand in your life."

He was talking of the past. Her parents had died within days of each other, taken by a fever. She was fourteen at the time and had left home to live with Colin Senior in Fort Benton. Her only sibling. He was nine years older, already married with a baby girl. But he'd welcomed her and given her a home.

But Austin had lost the right to share memories when he rode away without so much as a word.

The trail bent around a big rock and she pretended a great interest in keeping her attention on the ground beneath her feet.

Austin's sharply indrawn breath and Rosie's choked back squeak drew Mae's attention away from the toes of her shoes.

A man stood before them, gun drawn.

She recognized him as one of the stagecoach robbers. Hadn't they ridden away? Why hadn't he gone with his partners? What more could he want? She had nothing of value except a few coins. Did he want Austin's supplies? That's where Colin sat. He could have the horse and everything on it except Colin. She measured the distance to her nephew's side. Could she make it before the robber shot?

She had no desire to be wounded. And dead meant the children were alone.

She'd wait for an opening; when it was safe.

"I knows who you is," the man said. "Ya might try and disguise yerself, but I'd know Aussie Wagoner anywhere after ya shot my brother. Gunman, I'm here to ta make ya pay."

Mae couldn't move. Couldn't breathe. Couldn't blink. Couldn't even swallow.

Gunman? He'd always been fast when he was Deputy Sherriff back in Fort Benton. But she'd never thought of him as a gunman.

Austin held out his arms. "I'm unarmed."

"Get yer pistol, gunman. We're gonna have it out."

"I'm not interested."

With a speed that startled and alarmed Mae, the man jumped forward and grabbed her, his arm around her neck, pressing against her throat. She struggled to free herself. Fought for breath as fear pounded against her temples.

"Let her go." Austin's voice carried cold, hard steel in every word.

"Not until ya do me the honor of putting on yer firearm." The foul-smelling man pressed his gun to Mae's temple.

Mae pulled against the arm across her. She stilled enough to look at Austin. He watched her captor, his eyes like winter soil. Cold. Forbidding. Her mouth grew dry. This was a side of Austin she'd never seen.

"Very well." His gaze came to her. "So long as you swear to let her go if I do."

"I swear on my brother's grave." His arm tightened around Mae's neck, but she didn't fight him as Austin went to the packhorse. He spoke to Colin. Turned to say something to Rosie who had grown white.

God, help us.

Whither shall I go from thy spirit? Or whither shall I

flee from thy presence? If I ascend up into heaven, thou art there: if I make my bed in hell, behold, thou art there. If I take the wings of the morning, and dwell in the uttermost parts of the sea; even there shall thy hand lead me, and thy right hand shall hold me.

Remember. She mouthed the word and hoped the children understood.

Austin pulled a gun belt from the saddlebag.

"Put it on." The words blasted past Mae's ear.

Remember God is with us. Be brave.

Before the next hour passed, someone was going to be dead. She didn't know who it would be. But her future looked very frightening.

4

Austin didn't know a man could have a red color fill his vision while his thoughts were as sharp and clear as the air above them. To see that man holding Mae, to see the way she struggled in vain against his arm and to look at the children, their faces pale with fear, twisted his insides so hard he struggled to breathe. He recognized the man as one of the rustlers who'd ridden away when the bullets started flying. One of the dead men had been his brother, if he was to believe what was said.

He held his gun belt. "Let her go."

"Let's see that belt around ya first."

A feral growl burned over Austin's lips.

The man chortled. "Hear it slows ya down to be angry."

"I heard anger can make you faster and more accurate." He spoke with a coldness that came from deep inside.

The man's eyes flickered.

Good. Give him something to worry about.

He did up the belt. Paused. "Better holster your gun. I'm counting on a fair fight." He bent to tie the leather cords around his leg, his gaze never leaving the other man. He knew better than to trust him and had no desire to be shot with his gun holstered.

"I'll be wanting to kill ya fair and square."

Austin heard a gasp but didn't shift his attention from his opponent. "I'm sorry the children have to see this."

"Do 'em good. Show them what life is like." He pushed Mae away.

She stumbled, then righted herself and rushed to the horses. She caught up the reins and, with the children still on their backs, pulled the animals a distance off the trail.

The man holstered his gun and curled his fingers. The sound of cracking knuckles skittered along Austin's nerves and then every muscle, every nerve, every thought calmed, centered on nothing but the man before him.

"Aussie Wagoner, prepare to meet yer maker." The man's hand went for his gun.

Austin's hand went for his and he whipped the gun out. He hesitated a moment, not wanting to shoot the man in front of the children. Not wanting to shoot him at all. He'd had more than enough of the whole business. He shifted his aim and squeezed the trigger.

The man's gun flew from his hand.

Austin jerked back as if a wild bull had hit him in the shoulder. Odd. He'd never had that much kickback before.

The man screamed. "My hand! Ya shot my hand!" A string of vile words burst from his mouth.

Austin kept his gun aimed toward the man. "I suggest you get on your horse and skedaddle before I change my mind about letting you go."

Holding his injured hand in the palm of the other, the man half-ran, half-stumbled past the boulder by the side of the road.

Austin focused on the place and then watched him galloping south.

Not until the horse and rider faded into the distance did he holster his gun and look at his left arm. A dark spot seeped out from under the lapels of his coat.

Mae looked at him, her eyes wide, her lips parted. She swallowed audibly. "Who was that?"

"I never heard his name. But he was involved in cattle rustling at the Big Sky Ranch where I was helping out." His voice was steady, but his jaw so tense it creaked with every word. It would take a few minutes to settle back to calmness.

"He said you shot a man."

The words slammed into him. She'd be recalling another time that she knew of. "I was helping the Mounties stop the rustlers." His shoulder hurt and he rubbed at it. He pulled his hand out and looked at it. It glistened red. He stared at his fingers.

"You're still a lawman?"

More like a hired gun, but he wasn't going to admit that to her. "I've always been on the right side of the law." He lowered his voice to a growl. "But the wrong side of humanity."

Mae glanced at his hand and then at his shirt front. "You've been shot." She sprang forward then, as if remembering the children, said, "You two stay there." She strode right up to him and turned back the front of his coat. "You need to take this off." She glanced around. "Come and sit on that rock so I can look at it."

"It's nothing." He brushed her hands away. He did not want her touching him. It would undo all the ground he had gained since he'd last seen her. So many nights he'd wakened from a dream in which she brushed her fingers over his arm or took his hand. And not all the dreams occurred while he was asleep.

"Nonsense. Do as I say." She caught his right arm and pulled him forward.

He should put up more of a resistance. Should shake her hand off and swing into the saddle. Ride away. Not that riding into the distance had ever made it possible to forget her. He didn't reckon he'd ever get her out of his mind. Nor, to be honest, did he want to?

But somehow she forced him to cross to the rock, although force was a mighty strong word for the gentle pressure she'd exerted on his arm. He guessed he'd have to blame his lack of backbone on the fact he'd been shot. For sure, his shoulder felt like someone stuck a hot poker into it. Remembering Mae's vow to use such a weapon on any man who offended her, he laughed. Maybe she was grateful someone else had done it for her.

She pushed him down to the rock and planted her hands on her hips. "It's funny to be shot?"

He sobered, though he could feel amusement warming his eyes. "It feels like you've done what you threatened."

Her eyebrows rose. "I don't recall saying I'd shoot you."

He reminded her of the hot poker.

"I'm afraid you can't blame me for this." She pushed his coat off and reached for the buttons on his shirt.

He knew the moment she realized what she was about to do.

She sucked in air. Her hands hovered several inches from his chest.

"You don't have to do this. I'll survive." His arm hurt like fury. And the wet spot on his chest continued to grow. "I have an old shirt in my bag. I'll press it to the wound." He started to rise.

She pushed him down. "You'll do no such thing." She bit her bottom lip.

He didn't wait for her to act but undid his buttons with his right hand.

She shoved the sleeve back.

He looked at the wound. Sure was a small hole for the amount of pain it caused. "Check and see if there's an exit wound."

She looked at his back, leaning over him so that her hair swept across his cheek.

The pain subsided. He closed his eyes and inhaled her lavender scent.

She straightened. "No exit wound."

Meant the shooter had poorly made bullets. At least Austin made sure his bullets would do the job they were supposed to do.

"Wait here," Mae said and hurried back to the horses.

"Is he going to die?" Colin asked.

"Not if I have anything to do about it."

"He's a gunman?" Rosie whispered. "Does that mean he's a bad man?"

"You heard him. He was helping the Mounties. So no, he isn't a bad man."

Austin wondered why she didn't leave him to manage on his own. Not that he'd allow her to ride away without him. But why didn't she tell the children what sort of man he was? Had been. Though it seems he couldn't outrun his past. And why was she helping him? It simply didn't make sense. Perhaps he wasn't thinking clearly. After all, being challenged to a gunfight was hard on a man's nerves. Being shot, even harder.

She dug through her satchel and pulled out a white garment. An underskirt, if he had to guess, and he eyed it with a curiosity that sent a rush of heat up his neck. Her back to him, she ripped it into strips then returned to him. She poured water from the canteen against the wound and mopped it up with some of the rag. And she talked. Like she was wound too tight.

"I don't know much about gunshot wounds. Nothing, in fact. Have never before seen one and certainly have never had occasion to tend one. Of course, as a teacher, I see my share of bumps and bruises. One time, a bigger lad took a dare from another boy and climbed to the barn roof and jumped off. Crazy thing to do. Worse was he didn't judge where he was going to land. He slipped on the wet grass, fell and hit his head on a rock. There was a lot of blood. So much…" She shivered. "But the doctor looked after him."

He watched her work and listened to her talk. Her touch as she swabbed up the blood was gentle, almost driving away the pain. Her voice soothed like a mother's lullaby. Which made him think of home.

"I wonder how Ma and Pa are doing."

Her hands stilled and she sat back. "That seems an odd thing to say. Are you planning on going back?"

"No, I guess not." He paid them a visit from time to time, but they all understood that as long as he was near home, there would be those wanting to engage him in a gunfight. "A person can't go back."

"'Remember not the former things, nor consider the things of old. Behold, I am doing a new thing; now it springs forth, do you not perceive it? I will make a way in the wilderness and rivers in the desert.' That's from Isaiah." She sounded distracted.

"Chapter forty-three."

Her head came up and she met his eyes, hers full of surprise.

He chuckled softly. "Living in my cabin provides plenty of time for reading."

"Of course." She returned her attention to the wound.

He wished she'd look at him again. Let him bask in the blue of her eyes. Dream of a welcoming smile on her lips. But there were things about the past that couldn't be forgotten. And he should know. Hadn't he tried with all his might for five years?

Mae folded some of the cloth to make a pad to cover the wound. Her fingers brushed along the inner side of his arm as she wound strips around his shoulder to hold the pad in place.

He closed his eyes and groaned.

"Sorry, I'm doing my best not to hurt you."

At least she thought the hole in his shoulder pained him. But that pain was nothing compared to the pain in his heart that refused to heal. He reached down for his shirt, intending to put it on.

She took it. "You must have a clean shirt in your things. Tell me where and I'll get it."

"That's not necessary." He hurried to his feet, returned to the horses, and drew a shirt from his packs. He slipped the sleeve over his injured arm before she could insist on helping. But then he struggled to get into the other sleeve.

She held the shirt so he could get his arm in, then drew it over his shoulders. She did the same with his coat. And he didn't protest. He saw she had mopped the blood off the inside of his coat and rubbed it semi-dry.

"Thanks. Let's move on."

But no one moved. He allowed himself to look directly at the children for the first time since he'd sent a bullet into the other man. Just as he suspected it would be, their eyes were wide with disbelief and horror.

Now they were seeing him for who he was. Or at least, how everyone thought he was.

Would no one ever believe that he didn't want to be a gunman?

Mae scrubbed her hands up and down the side of her skirt. Not that it did anything to ease the way they shook. She gritted her teeth, determined not to let shivers overtake her body. The children had witnessed enough without seeing her turn into a quivering mass of nerves.

She'd always known of Austin's reputation. After all, that's why the sheriff hired him. But to see someone challenge him was like having the ground snatched from under her feet. He obviously didn't like killing or he would have shot the man through the heart, not simply disarmed him. That was more than she ever wanted to witness. But to see him shot! Well, there weren't words to describe the jolt that raced through her own body and robbed her of anything but a silent scream.

She pressed her fingers to the sides of her legs, forcing them to steadiness.

They'd held hands and hugged and kissed when they were courting; but never had she seen him with his shirt off. Never had she touched his bare chest.

Her throat tightened. Her heart hammered against her ribcage. He was a big man. His chest was muscular. His shoulder the sort a woman could lean on both figuratively and literally.

If not for the urgency of tending his wound, she might have run her fingers along his collar bone.

Her cheeks burned at the boldness of her thoughts.

Austin reached for the reins. But instead of leading the horses back to the trail, he looked up at the children.

"I'm sorry you had to see that. The man was wrong. That sort of thing isn't the way life is. Life is full of flowers and birds, sunshine and warm breezes." He lifted his head to the sky. "And yes, snow."

Mae looked upward. The air was cold, but did he think it would snow? It seemed early, but it was late November. Before they left Montana they'd already had early snows that had melted.

Tears ran down Rosie's face.

Colin's eyes were so wide she wondered if he could even blink.

"The children need some comforting before we move on." She reached up for Rosie.

The girl fell into her arms and clung to her, sobbing quietly.

Austin reached up with his good arm and lifted Colin down. But Colin wrapped his arms around Austin's neck and wouldn't let go.

"Be careful of his arm," Mae warned.

"My arm is fine." Austin held Colin, bending his head to the little guy's tangled blond hair.

Austin moved to Mae's side. "I'm sorry any of you had to see that. I wish..." He didn't finish.

She wanted to say something, but her thoughts were tangled. Did she want him to explain why he was a gunman? Or tell him all that mattered was he hadn't been seriously hurt? Or ask the question that burned a permanent scar in her brain? Why had he left her? Was it to pursue a life of fast shooting? On the right side of the law, as he'd been careful to explain.

Austin sighed. "I wish life was different."

Colin leaned back to look into Austin's face. "Different? How?"

"I wish bad things didn't happen. I wish everyone could be happy and content. I wish..." He shrugged.

Rosie looked up and smiled through her tears. "Aunt Mae says bad things are like rain. Rain makes flowers grow. And bad things make us grow into a stronger, better person."

Austin looked at Mae, his smile emphasizing the fan lines from his eyes. "Your aunt is very wise."

"That's because she's a teacher," Colin said.

Amusement flashed in Austin's eyes and echoed in Mae's heart. They both chuckled.

Austin glanced past Mae. "The day is passing. We need to make some miles. Are you two...three...ready to move on?"

She looked at the position of the sun. Halfway down the afternoon sky. "We're ready."

He took Colin back to the packhorse while she took Rosie to the other animal. Before Rosie could scramble aboard, Austin came to Mae's side and held his hand against his knee for her to use to mount.

"You're injured. You need to ride."

"I'm fine."

"No, you're not. You have a gunshot wound right there." She jabbed toward the site. "I expect it's still bleeding, so you're the one who should ride."

They stared at each other, neither giving in.

"Time's passing," she said.

He sighed. "Are you always this stubborn?"

"You can't make progress in life if you let someone push you aside."

He snorted. "I'm not pushing anyone." He bent over again. "Now mount up."

She didn't move. "Listen. I'll ride if you ride." It was a decent compromise.

He straightened and studied the horses. "I'm too much weight for the packhorse. And riding atop the packs is more than I expect from you."

"Don't misjudge me. I'm capable of doing hard things."

They studied each other, taking stock. She couldn't say what he sought or what he saw, but she looked for answers he'd never given her and an understanding of who this man was.

"Time's wasting." He took the reins of Colin's horse

and started down the road, leaving her standing beside the other horse, Rosie at her side.

"Auntie, we've got to keep up."

"I know." The words came out on a frustrated sigh. "You get up." She helped Rosie to the saddle, then took the reins and walked after the others.

"Are you going to walk?" Rosie was clearly confused about what was going on.

Well she might be. So was Mae. All she knew was that Austin ought to ride. And so long as he wasn't, neither would she. And it wasn't simply stubbornness, though no doubt he was thinking that. Yes, she was concerned about his wound and for that reason alone, he should ride. But he'd done things his way once, leaving her without a word of explanation and it felt like if she gave in to him on this occasion, then she was saying it was fine for him to have done that.

She smirked. It was a good thing no one asked her to explain her muddled thoughts.

They caught up to the other horse.

Austin frowned at her, his eyebrows drawing together. "Why are you walking?"

With perfect calm, she said, "So I can catch you when you fall over."

He snorted then laughed. "I outweigh you by a hundred pounds or more. I can't see you being able to catch me."

She shrugged. "Then maybe you should save your energy and ride."

"I am not going to ride while you walk." He spoke each word through gritted teeth.

"Fine." She took the reins from him before he could think to stop her, led the packhorse toward a good-sized rock. She stood on the rock, grabbed the ropes on the saddle packs and by sheer determination, pulled herself up behind Colin. Austin was right. The packs were uncomfortable to sit on. But she'd never admit it. Not in a hundred years.

"Rosie, get behind the saddle," she called.

Rosie squirmed herself into place.

Mae looked at Austin. "Are you going to get on your horse or stand there staring while the sun heads west?"

He scowled. He grunted. He looked past her and sighed long. Then he went to the horse and pulled himself into the saddle, rode closer, took up the rope of the packhorse and without a word, continued down the road.

"Is he mad at us?" Colin asked after a few minutes, his voice low, as if fearing Austin would hear.

Mae recalled something that had happened years ago when she and Austin were good friends. She'd taken a fall. Nothing serious. But he was upset. Said he thought she'd taken an unnecessary chance trying to jump over the tree trunk when she could have climbed over and not put herself at risk. For twenty minutes he didn't say another word until she finally asked if he was angry.

The way he'd drawn in air made her think he'd been holding his breath since his last word. And then he spoke so softly and gently that she barely heard him. "I don't care for seeing you hurt, but I'm not angry."

"Then what is it?"

"The depth of my feelings for you scares me."

At the time she'd understood. Her own feelings for him were so big that sometimes they threatened to consume her. What happened to those feelings? Hers had been stuffed back time and again until there had formed a tenuous barrier holding them back.

But what happened to steal away the feelings he had for her?

Colin waited for her answer to his question. "I don't think he's angry."

"Then why isn't he talking?"

She thought she knew the answer. At least if he was anything like the man she remembered. "I think perhaps he is worried about getting us to a safe place." She spoke loud enough for him to hear.

He jerked as if yanked unexpectedly from his thoughts. "I will keep you safe if my life depends on it."

Her feelings were mixed to think he was still the caring, protective man she remembered.

"Does that mean he's gonna die?" Colin's voice was shrill.

Austin's laugh was dry. "Not if I can help it. We'll all reach town or the ranch in one piece."

"Except you have a hole in your arm." Rosie leaned against Austin, her arms around him.

Mae knew she would be holding on tight. But not for her sake. For his. Her young niece was trying to comfort and help Austin.

They moseyed on, keeping the pace slow for the sake of the horses. They climbed several hills, allowing them a sweeping view of valleys and more hills.

She noticed Austin studying their surroundings. Did he know where they were?

"Are you familiar with this road?" she asked.

"Been over it once before. I know where it goes."

"Where is that?"

"To Fort Calgary."

"I thought we were headed for Logan Crossing." Had he misled her?

"Logan Crossing is a bit off the main road, but we'll see the turn-off when we get to it."

That didn't answer her question as to what he was looking for. "Are you expecting to see something out there?" She felt the children's interest and prayed his answer would be reassuring.

"I heard there are other ranches along these hills. I

was hoping we'd see one where we could spend the night."

The night! She hadn't considered they wouldn't reach a town before dark. And if they didn't? She knew the answer. They could either continued to ride or camp.

Either way, she'd be forced to spend the night with a man she wasn't married to. It would be frowned upon and judged no matter what the circumstances.

Just when she thought she would get a place where she and the children could settle in for a spell. She knew there was no way a teacher would be allowed any excuse for such lax behavior.

5

Austin scanned the view, searching for any sign of human habitation. He'd heard there were several small ranchers along the hills. Had taken note of their approximate location. It never hurt to be properly informed. Once, he saw a movement in the distance, but it turned out to be a moose. Nothing that offered a place to spend the night.

Sleeping outside didn't bother him in the least, but he wasn't sure how Mae and the children would manage. Could he keep them warm and dry? He glanced toward the sky. There was no sign of another storm. But more than that, where had that man he shot gone, and where were his accomplices?

"You see anything?" Rosie asked. Her arms hugged him. She pressed to his back. It was rather a comforting feeling to have her there, holding him tight. Though, of course, she was holding herself tight. He knew it, but it still felt good.

"Just hills and sky." He had no intention of informing her of all his worries. The least he could do, seeing as he'd brought so much evil into her life, was to protect her from any more.

He glanced over his shoulder to check on Mae and Colin.

She noticed him turn and smiled and nodded her head. No doubt wanting him to believe she was as comfortable as if she sat in a worn rocking chair.

Turning reminded him of the hole in his shoulder.

"You ever been shot before?" Rosie asked.

"First time."

"Why'd you let him shoot you?"

"Let him?" As if he'd asked the man to do it.

"You were faster than him. I saw it. You could have shot him better."

By better, he guessed she meant through the heart. "It's not easy to shoot a man."

"But he's a bad man."

"I suppose he is."

The silence between them lengthened. Perhaps she'd decided to let the subject end.

"Mr. Austin, why do you shoot people?"

Her innocent concern ached clear through him. She should never have witnessed the gunplay. Life should be sweet and gentle for children. "Good question. Mostly it's to help others or to stay alive."

Her head bumped against his back as if she nodded. "Auntie says that people who live by the gun die by the gun."

Austin glanced back. From the look on Mae's face, he knew she heard the entire conversation. He held her gaze for a heartbeat, then turned his attention back to the trail before he answered.

"There's another option. Put aside the guns and live a long, peaceful life."

"I like that." She seemed content and they rode in silence.

The sun dipped toward the west. Cold air seeped across the land.

He squinted into the distance. Not one sign of a homestead. He dropped back to the side of the other horse. "It will soon be dark and cold. I think we should make camp and spend the night."

Mae didn't look at him, but Colin grinned like it was the best news he'd heard in days. Austin remembered when he'd been that eager for adventure and excitement.

He waited for Mae to agree to his suggestion. Not that she had much choice. Even if the horses were up to riding through the night, it was dangerous.

Again, he scanned the view in every direction. Was

that man out there still seeking revenge? Were his companions with him?

He mentally weighed the options and stopping for the night still seemed the better of some very poor choices.

Finally, Mae nodded. "We need to think about the children and the horses."

"Follow me." He led the way down a gentle slope to the side of a stream. Rosie slid off and then Austin dismounted, ignoring the painful protest in his left arm, and went to assist Mae from the packhorse.

"I can manage." She slid from the animal. She clung to the ropes for a moment as Colin swung down, then she faced him, her face set in determined lines.

"You don't convince me," Austin said. "I know you are sore and stiff in places you didn't know existed."

"Then I guess we're even."

"How's that?" How could she being sore equal in any way the pain of shooting her brother?

"You don't convince me your arm isn't bothering you."

Oh, that. "It's nothing I can't live with." He resisted cradling his elbow to take pressure off his shoulder.

"Doesn't appear you have much choice unless you plan to sit down and die."

He laughed at her dry tone. "Nope. That's not part of my plan."

"Then what is, if I may ask?" She glanced around

the area then brought her gaze to him, watching…waiting.

"I…um…" But why did she care that he meant to return to his cabin? Besides, hadn't he made that clear? Then he realized she meant immediate plans. "We'll build a fire to keep us warm and cook some food. We'll build a little shelter for the night." He remembered the tarpaulin was wet. Now would be a good time to get it out and let it dry.

Untying the saddle packs proved to be a challenge. His left arm hurt like fury when he used it.

Mae came to his side. "I'll help."

Seems 'help' meant doing it herself. But he knew the packs were too heavy for her and he lifted them with one arm and parked them where he thought they should build their camp. Near enough to the trees to provide shelter. Close to the water to make it easy to dip from the stream.

Mae called out to the children. "Gather up some firewood. Mind you don't wander far. It will soon be dark."

Austin realized he should have thought of that first. Too late now. He knelt and took the tarp. "I'm going to tie a rope from that tree to that one and hang the tarp over it. It will provide us some shelter and hopefully dry." He took a length of rope to the first tree. He grunted as he tried to tie the knots.

Again, Mae stepped forward and reached around him to help.

Again, her hair brushed his cheek, making him forget every thread of pain.

She stepped back and carried the end of the rope to the second tree and tied it there. She helped him drape the canvas over the rope.

They stood back, side by side.

"I remember that about you." His voice had a deep note to it. Would she hear it and put it down to pain rather than to the grip of his memories?

"What do you remember?"

"How you always helped others."

"I don't recall."

"There was the time Mrs. Allen couldn't find her basket and you retraced her steps until you found it outside the store. You said she must have set it down and forgotten it."

"Poor Mrs. Allen was a little forgetful."

"A little? Seems to me she sometimes got lost going from her garden to her house."

"She was a gentle soul."

That was another thing he remembered about Mae. She found kind excuses for people's behavior and often overlooked things others found annoying or off-putting. Maybe that was why she wasn't taking a hot poker to him.

"I remember another time at a church picnic. They

needed someone to organize activities for the children. You were with your friends—" Did he remember her enjoying the attention of a young man? But that was before he started to court her. The fellow had been forgotten in the following days. "You left your friends and organized all sorts of games."

"Good practice for being a teacher." She straightened the tarp at one corner, then looked at him, her gaze direct and, it seemed to him, accusing. "Do I recall you assisting with the games?"

"I guess I did." He hadn't forgotten. Not one single moment. "That's when I decided I wanted to cour—" He broke off. No point in reminding either of them that after that he'd begun to court her. That was water under the bridge.

Thankfully, the children returned, their arms full of deadfall. Ignoring the pain in his arm that faded in comparison to the pain in his heart, he built a fire and heated some canned meat and bean soup he'd purchased at the fort. He found enough containers for everyone and shared the loaf of bread he'd purchased. There'd be no more bread until he reached his cabin and made his own.

Before they ate, he said he'd say grace. He bowed his head. "Our Father who art in heaven, thank you for protecting each one here. Keep us safe through the night and thank you for the food. Amen."

Colin had the first spoonful to his mouth before Austin lifted his head.

He grinned at Mae. She watched her nephew, a pleased look on her face. Austin's shoulders sagged. She'd loved her brother every bit as much. She'd told him how her parents had died and Colin Senior was her only relative and he'd gladly given her a home.

He realized Colin asked him a question. "What was that?"

"Where are we gonna sleep?"

"Right here. Between the fire and the tarpaulin."

"Really?"

"Unless you have a better suggestion."

Colin's head rocked back and forth. "That's the best idea. Aunt Mae will never let me sleep outside. She says it isn't safe." He made a scoffing noise. "She thinks I'm scared of a mouse."

Rosie giggled. "Cause she knows you are."

"Am not."

Rosie ducked her head.

Austin was impressed that Rosie didn't pursue teasing her brother.

Mae gathered up the empty dishes. "Let's take these to the river to wash." She and Rosie headed in that direction. Colin didn't move.

"Colin, you too," Mae called.

"But Austin isn't going," the boy protested.

"Maybe because he's got a gunshot wound." Rosie's voice rang with defense.

"I'll come," Austin said. "We need the canteens filled."

The four of them went the few yards to the stream. They washed the dishes and filled the canteens, then stood watching the sunset pour color into the water. Orange and pink and purple in bands of color. "The colors move as if directed by an unseen hand," he said.

"God's," Rosie said.

"You're right. In Genesis, it says, 'And God said, Let there be light: and there was light. And God saw the light, that it was good: and God divided the light from the darkness. And God called the light Day, and the darkness he called Night. And the evening and the morning were the first day.'" Austin couldn't imagine why he felt he needed to quote those verses.

Mae spoke softly. "And everything that God made He said was good."

No matter what the future held for Austin, even if he spent the rest of his life alone in the mountains, this moment would stay with him. A holy blessed feeling.

Shadows grew long and heavy. The fire behind them flared, sending sparks upward. A signal to anyone trying to find them.

He returned to the camp site. Stared at the fire. If he was alone, he would have quenched it, but without the warmth, the others would be cold. He patted the gun at his side. He'd keep it handy until they reached safety. At least his right arm was in good shape.

He stowed the dishes and handed two blankets and his ground sheet to Mae. He had bedding for one. Not four. "You'll have to huddle together."

"We'll be fine." Mae spread the ground sheet, covered the children with the blankets, then sat beside them, her hand to Rosie's shoulder as if adding her warmth to the meager covers.

"You could crawl in beside them."

She kept her attention on the dancing flames. "You didn't keep any blankets for yourself. What will you do?"

"I'll stay by the fire. It's warm here." Thankfully, his coat provided protection from the cold sifting down the hill and blowing at the flames.

"I'll do the same."

Running low on patience, he sighed long and hard, the movement tugging at his shoulder. He gritted his teeth and waited for the pain to ease before he spoke. "Mae, I am dressed for the weather. More than that, I am used to dealing with the cold. So, don't play the suffering hero with me." His words were sharper, more condemning than he meant. "I'm sorry. I didn't mean to sound harsh. It's just that I don't see any need for you to endure the cold."

"I'm not content to let you suffer because of us."

He studied the words. Rolled them over in his mind

several times. Did she mean she cared? But how could she? It must mean something else, but he couldn't find a reason she might be concerned for his well-being. Except for one thing. She needed him to help her get to a town or ranch. Or did she? If he wasn't there…like, for instance, he was dead…couldn't she take the horses and continue on? All she had to do was follow the trail.

Nope. She had no need of him.

No reason to be concerned about him.

So why was she?

It baffled him and he didn't care for the feeling. It sat in his brain with the same burning intensity as the hole in his shoulder.

"Austin, stop trying to figure out a way to make me ignore you."

He tried not to sputter his protest. "I'm not."

"Good." She moved closer to him. "How's your shoulder?"

"Which one?"

She bumped his right arm with her elbow. "Not this one."

He would ignore her question but guessed she would continue until she got an answer. "Hurts some. Don't know why."

She gave a short chuckle. "I can't imagine why a little gunshot wound should hurt."

"It shouldn't." And he wished it didn't. Shouldn't

the pain be abating? Instead, it burned like the fire had taken residence there.

"Is it still bleeding?" she asked.

"Nope." The pad was dry and crusty. And that was probably the reason the wound hurt more. He should remove the offending bandage. But he didn't bother. Took too much effort. "Colin reminds me of myself when I was that age."

"Really, in what way?"

"Well, to start with, he's a boy. Though his hair is blond while mine was always brown."

He guessed Mae's quiet sigh meant she knew he wasn't answering her question. "I was so eager for adventure. Couldn't wait for what Beecher had planned next."

"I remember you telling me about your brother. Wasn't he four years older than you?"

"Yes, he was. And he was afraid of nothing. Despite Ma and Pa's warnings against it, he had a fondness for guns." Why was he telling her this? Did he hope to justify himself in her eyes? "They didn't like him teaching me how to shoot, so we did it away from the house. Beecher was fast and liked to challenge others. At first, it was shooting targets. But then someone told him that was too easy. Try out drawing a man face-to-face. Beecher refused until he was called out in the street one day and had to defend himself." Austin shivered. "You're right. Those who live by the gun die by the gun."

"He was shot? You never told me that."

"It's not something I like to talk about."

"How old were you?"

He shivered again at the power of that memory. "I was sixteen. I watched him die in the street, blood pooling on his chest."

Mae rested her hand on his arm. "Austin, that must have been awful. I know how much you loved your brother. I am so sorry."

"It doesn't change anything." She'd loved her brother too. "I thought I could somehow make him proud of me by following in his footsteps. But I never cared for shooting people."

"So you hide out in the mountains."

His short laugh was mirthless. "With my wooden and wild animal friends." He shivered again and reached over to put more wood on the fire. "You better get some sleep. Don't know what tomorrow holds."

"Where are you sleeping?"

"Right here. Close to the fire." The fire seemed strangely lacking in warmth. Must be the breeze brushing his back and stealing away any warmth. Mae would be feeling the same thing. He moved toward the children, finding more protection under the tarpaulin. Maybe that would help.

Mae sat beside her niece and nephew. Too stubborn to lay down.

It had been a long day. Austin was tired clear through to his core. He tipped over to his right side and let sleep claim him.

The flames danced against his eyelids. Growing taller and taller until they took the form of a man. Austin couldn't make out the man's features, but he was almost certain it was one of the stagecoach robbers. Austin moaned, tried to call out to Mae to take the children and run, but he couldn't make his way through the fog. Couldn't make his words clear. Couldn't waken Mae.

Were they doomed to die out here?

Not if he could do anything and he reached for his gun.

MAE SAT UP, wakened by a sound. She shivered, more from nerves than cold. She rubbed the sleep from her eyes and looked around. Her nerves settled when she didn't see any wild beast or strange men. But the sound came again. From Austin. He must be dreaming. Or if his moans meant anything, having a nightmare.

She moved closer and nudged him gently. "Austin, wake up."

He jerked upright, his gun in his hand, aimed directly at her.

Her heart spasmed so hard she thought it might have ruptured and at the same time, she threw herself to the ground.

"Austin, it's me! Mae!" Surely the name must mean something even in his half-awake, half-asleep state. "It's me, Mae," she said again. "Put your gun down."

He shook his head as if forcing himself from sleep. He lowered his hand a fraction.

She had to get the gun before he aimed at her again and gently reached for it.

He gripped it harder.

"Austin, let me take it. Austin." She spoke louder, firmer, like a good school teacher, hoping he would snap out of his condition. She gently lifted each of his fingers until she could take the gun from his hand. She set it aside, shuddering at how close she had come to being shot.

She sat up and edged closer. "Austin, are you awake?" She nudged his shoulder.

He was shivering.

"You're freezing. Come closer to the fire." She tossed on more wood. She pulled on his arm, trying to make him move nearer the warmth.

A shudder shook him and he expelled a long breath. He looked at her and blinked. "Mae? What are you doing here?"

Was he confused from sleep? Or was he fevered from the gunshot? She almost reached out her hand to touch his forehead, but remembering his reaction to her waking him, she decided it wasn't worth the risk. Even without him having his gun. "There was a stagecoach robbery. Remember?"

"Of course. I was dreaming and thought—never mind. Is everyone all right?" He glanced toward the children who had, thankfully, slept through the incident.

"We're fine."

"Good. We'll move on as soon as there is light. They'll come tomorrow."

Her jaw creaked. Was he still confused? "Who?"

"They'll send someone out to look for the stagecoach."

"That's good to know." She sat down, her knees drawn up at an angle so she could watch Austin, still not convinced he wasn't going to shoot her or someone. She was tired but would not go to sleep.

Austin patted his right hip. "Where's my gun?" He leaped to his feet, urgency ringing from his words.

Mae was on her feet just as quickly and went to where she'd put the gun. She scooped it up. "Austin, I took it from you. You almost shot me. I think I should keep it until morning."

The firelight made his features hard and shadowed. His eyes narrowed. His mouth tightened. "Do you know how to shoot? Could you shoot someone if they threatened you or the children?" His voice was devoid of warmth.

"I'll protect the children." She knew the steps of firing a gun, though she'd never actually done it. Colin Senior had often said she should learn, but she'd never had any desire to do so and after he was shot to death, she had even less.

"I think I better have the gun." He held out his hand.

She shook her head and backed away. "Do you often have nightmares and wake up wanting to shoot someone?"

"Can't say as I do."

She put her hands and the gun behind her back. "Guess there's a first time for everything. I really don't care for being the target for your bullet."

His hands dropped to his side. He swallowed loudly. "Mae, I would never intentionally hurt you. Surely you know that."

"Your reflexes are too fast. I'm afraid they'll get ahead of your intentions. I'll keep the gun." Even though she really didn't care to have it in her possession.

Even in the undulating light, she saw the hard set of his jaw. Knew he wasn't going to give in. But then, neither was she. Her heart still hadn't resumed its normal pace. She might have been shot. What if one of the children startled him in the night. No, she wasn't going to let him have his gun.

Nor was she prepared to stand there and argue with him the rest of the night. She moved back to the children, sat beside them, and put the gun under her knees. He'd have to dig under her skirts to get it and somehow she didn't think he'd stoop to doing that.

At least not the Austin she remembered.

But how well did she know him? The man she thought she knew would never have ridden away without telling her and giving her a reason.

All the more reason to keep the gun in her possession.

Austin muttered something under his breath. She didn't ask him to repeat himself.

He stared at her. She could feel his gaze burning at her, but she ignored him. She had no idea how long until morning would come, but there was no sign of dawn. "Austin, you might as well get some rest."

He crossed his arms and stood between her and the fire. Orange and yellow flared around him.

"You look like some monster rising from the flames," she said. "Go sit down." She used her best teacher voice. Kind, yet firm, informing him she would brook no argument.

He sat a few feet away. "You're different than I remember."

"A person grows up in five years. And having two children to take care of does tend to change a person."

"Harrumph."

She couldn't let it pass. "You're different too."

"How?"

She smiled at his defensiveness. He was more like Colin than he realized. "You would have never pointed a gun at me back then."

"I didn't know it was you. I thought I saw the man who shot me." He paused a moment. "And I didn't intend to let him shoot me or you or the children."

His words might have been more comforting if she hadn't seen the wrong side of his gun.

He shivered. How could he still be cold with the flames throwing heat for ten feet and then the canvas bouncing it back? She considered the events of the past few minutes. His confusion. His confession that he didn't normally have nightmares. Was it possible he had developed an infection in his wound? Was there even time for that to have happened? But infection would certainly explain his odd behavior. But then, how did she know it wasn't perfectly normal for him? And yet somehow she didn't think it was. Yes, infection would account for many things.

And would certainly complicate getting to safety.

"Austin, how are you feeling?"

"Naked without my gun."

"Well, I can tell you that you aren't naked." Her

cheeks burned at the thought. "You are dressed and in your right mind. Or not."

His head jerked up. "You think I'm not in my right mind?"

"You were mumbling in your sleep and threatened to shoot me."

"I told you. I thought I saw that man."

"Where did you see him?"

"In my sleep, I guess." He shook his head. "Very well, I admit it. I was having a nightmare. But I'm fine now." He lay down and curled up on his side. "And I'm going to sleep. You should too."

"I will." But she remained seated, watching Austin. What if he got delirious and got aggressive? She wouldn't be able to control him.

Sleep was impossible after that thought.

She woke to someone patting her arm.

"Rosie, what is it?"

"Look at Austin," she whispered.

Mae sat up so suddenly her head spun. She hadn't meant to fall asleep. She felt around for the gun and released an anxious breath when she found it still under her skirt.

Austin lay on his back, his arms at his side, snoring up a storm.

"How did I sleep through that?" she whispered to

Rosie as she glanced back to see where Colin was.

He slept on his back, his arms at his side, the blanket tossed to one side. He didn't quite snore, but he snuffled.

She grinned at how alike Colin and Austin were. "Thank goodness we are more ladylike when we sleep." She kept her voice very low.

Rosie pressed a hand to her mouth to still her giggles.

Coals still glowed on the fire and Mae tossed on more wood.

Austin snorted, waking himself up.

Mae kept a close eye on him, uncertain what to expect.

He shifted to his side and watched her. His eyes were gentle. No sign of last night's confusion. Perhaps it had simply been a reaction to the encounter with that man. After all, she thought with a touch of humor, it wasn't every day someone tried to shoot you. Or was it? She didn't know.

Had she ever thanked him for defending her? She couldn't remember.

He sat up, yawned and stretched. Grunting as he moved his left arm.

"Sore, is it?"

"Hurts a little all right." He patted his holster. "You still got my gun?"

"I don't have it on me." She'd left it on the ground.

Maybe not the smartest thing to do, considering Colin's curiosity about all things. She resisted looking in that direction, not wanting Austin to know where she'd left it.

But he took two long strides over and picked it up. He put it in the gun belt, untied and unbuckled the belt, and stowed it in the saddle bags. She noted that he used his left arm very little.

Mae nodded, relieved to have the gun out of sight and out of his reach. She glanced up the hill and along the stream. What if someone came after them? One of those stagecoach robbers?

No, it was better to have it put away. Besides, the man who'd shot Austin wouldn't be using his hand for a while. He was undoubtedly off somewhere, licking his wounds.

"Now let's see to breakfast," Austin said.

He set a pot of water between some rocks over the fire and soon had cornmeal mush simmering. He even produced a bottle of syrup to sweeten it.

Colin chattered non-stop. Commenting on how to cook over a fire, informing them all he meant to learn, then suddenly shifting his conversation to observations about the birds in the trees. "Most of the birds have gone south," he said with a degree of pride in knowing that. He told Austin about the school where they were going.

"It's brand new. Auntie will be the first teacher

there. She says if everything goes well, we might live there for a long time."

Mae's food stuck in her throat and she coughed. It wouldn't be long when her employers discovered that she'd spent the night with Austin. Though it was of necessity and they have behaved seemingly. The facts would make no difference in the minds of others.

"I've met some of the people there."

Austin's comment drew her attention.

"There was a man and a woman and two little boys. Strange story it was. The boys had been kept captive by their uncle. The uncle had kidnapped the young woman because her father was rich. The young man… well, I don't recall how he ended up in the story, though I can tell you that he is now forever a part of their story. You see, the young man and young woman got married as soon as they reached the fort."

They probably weren't given a choice, Mae thought, a sour taste in her mouth.

"How'd they get away from the bad man?" Colin asked.

"The uncle decided they must all go with him to the fort where he meant to trade the woman for her ransom money."

"He was a very bad man," Rosie's voice rang with conviction.

"Some say he got what he deserved. He drowned on the way out. They'd all fallen into the river. The others got out and were making their way to the fort when I found them and helped them."

"So the story has a happy ending?" Rosie's tone begged to know it had.

"From what I hear, they are very happy. The man and woman love each other very much and the two little boys have a new mama and papa who love them."

Mae got to her feet. "We need to get moving." She took the dishes to the stream to wash.

Austin followed with the canteens and filled them. "Did I say something wrong?" He must think her sudden departure meant he had.

The children carried water to douse the fire.

She gathered up the now clean dishes. "No, course not. It's just that not all stories can have such a happy ending."

"I know that. But you're headed to a good place. You and the children will do well there.

"That was my goal. My dream." She returned to the camp, folded the blankets, untied the ropes, and helped Austin fold the tarp. At least it was now dry.

She helped him get the horses ready. Guessed it was a sign of how much his wound pained that he let her.

Colin declared he liked riding on the packhorse and pulled himself up there.

"You ride with Rosie today," Austin said.

"Are we going to do this again?"

"What?"

"I refuse to ride while you walk." She made no move toward either horse.

Nor did he.

"Very well, if that's how you want it." She would not waste time arguing. "Rosie, get on the horse." She helped the girl mount, grabbed the reins and marched down the road leading the horse.

"You're more stubborn than I remember." Austin took the packhorse's rope and walked beside Mae.

"Life has required I be determined."

"How so?"

"I have two children to take care of. That means I sometimes have to confront people who think I can't do a good job."

"Of teaching or mothering?"

"Both. Though most are content to let me raise the children." The injustices of her last few positions filled her mind with fire. "I disciplined students because they needed it. Sometimes their little Johnnys or Sarahs were not the sweet angels they would have others think. I didn't have to discipline Colin or Rosie as much because they are well behaved."

"I noticed that."

She slowed her breathing, calmed her anger. "All I asked was to be judged by the facts, but facts hold little weight against offended parents."

"But now you can start over."

She clamped her teeth together and didn't point out that she would again be judged unfairly. It was Austin's fault. Except it wasn't. Nor would she say anything and make him think she expected him to marry her. Heavens above. That was the last thing she wanted. A marriage based on guilt, not love. She'd obviously not been enough five years ago and very little had changed.

The morning sun grew warm. Austin shrugged from his coat and hung it on the saddle.

She glanced at his shirt. "Looks like you might still be bleeding."

"I'm fine."

"If you say so." She wasn't about to waste her time arguing with a stubborn man.

They settled into silence. Dust kicked up from their feet. The trail rose before them and they walked up the incline. By the time they reached the top, she was out of breath and stopped a moment. Thankfully, Austin didn't mention that she was slowing them down.

She turned, prepared to say thank you when he crumpled to the ground.

With a cry of surprise, she ran to his side. "Austin, what happened?" She touched his forehead and knew the answer.

He was burning up with fever.

Rosie and Colin rushed to her side.

"What's wrong with him?" Rosie asked.

"He's sick."

"He gonna die?" Colin asked, tears pooling in his eyes.

"I certainly hope not."

Austin's eyes opened. "I'm fine." His words lacked clarity.

"You most certainly are not fine." She looked around. If he could get to the trees at the side of the road she could…what? The only water they had was in the three canteens. She wasn't even sure she could start a fire. She had no idea of where they were. Nor where she might find help.

"God, help us," she prayed.

6

"Can you stand?" The words echoed through Austin's head.

Mae sounded so concerned about such a basic thing. Of course, he could stand. Did she think he was a baby? Except his legs seemed to have disconnected from the rest of him. His arm hurt. His head thundered like a raging storm.

He tried again to get his feet under him. Why did he have to lean so heavily on Mae? He was too big. Weighed too much for her. And yet she was all that kept him from crashing face forward into the dirt.

She helped him sit with his back to a tree.

"I'm as weak as a baby," he grumbled.

"You're sick." She unbuttoned his shirt and eased the blood-soaked pad from his shoulder. "Pus. You have an infection."

The sound of worry in her voice brought his thoughts into focus. He reached for her hand. "Mae, don't worry about me. I'll be fine."

"Of course you will. Because you say so and that's enough."

He heard the sharpness in her tone but knew it was because she worried. Because she cared. He knew the latter wasn't possible, but he wanted to believe it at the moment. "Where are we?"

"Here."

"Very funny."

"I have no idea where we are. But I'll do my best to take care of this wound."

"Couldn't ask for more."

She gave a mirthless chuckle. "Oh, we certainly could. We could ask for a doctor or at least a home with water and medication." She sighed. "But you're stuck with me."

"I'm glad." The words seemed to come from a long, dark tunnel.

"You sit back while I do what I can."

"Hadn't figured on getting up and running away." He forced his thoughts to stay present when they wanted to wander off. "Where are the children?"

"They're taking care of the horses."

Before he could form a protest, she continued.

"It will keep them busy. I didn't care for them to hang over my shoulder and ask questions."

"Umm." It took too much effort to bring a word to his mouth.

"This might hurt." She dribbled water on his wound and then pressed on it.

He reared up. "Darn tootin' that hurts."

She pushed him back against the tree. "I have to get the infection out. What did that man do? Dip the bullet in something foul before he used it? I wouldn't put it past him. To my dismay, I have learned there are all sorts of people in this world. Some who are very evil. Also, some who are good and kind. I wish there were more of the latter."

Her words washed over him. Distracting him from the pain. Probably why she babbled on like a rushing stream.

"I mean, is it too much to ask for honesty? And faithfulness? Not to mention commitment. Really. Wouldn't life be a lot more pleasant for everyone if those few attributes were practiced? How hard is it to choose good over bad?" She huffed, drawing a weak smile from Austin.

She huffed again. "Take those men and their wives who are on school boards. Not just one, mind you. Four different locations at last count. The wives complain. Say unkind things. Tell their husbands that a teacher can't have children of her own because it's unfair to the other children. You know what's unfair? Being accused of favoritism when I bent over backward to make sure I didn't treat my own niece and nephew any differently. There was simply no way to win against such accusations. It was so unfair." She swabbed at his wound with a wet cloth, then sat back on her heels. "I'm not sure what else I can do. Austin, how am I to get you to a place where you can be doctored?"

The concern in her voice drew his attention. He lifted his good arm and touched her shoulder. "They will come."

"Who?" Her voice was sharp.

"They'll look for the stagecoach."

"Oh yes. I'd forgotten that."

He felt her shoulders sag.

"So much as happened since we left the fort that I feel like it's been a week." Her voice carried a note of awe.

"Glad I could be of help." Not that she'd thanked him for rescuing her, but nevertheless he had and he was grateful for the opportunity. "I wish things had turned out differently." If only he hadn't been the one to stop Colin Senior with a bullet. He would have followed his heart and asked her to marry him. He'd had every confidence that she would have agreed.

Rosie and Colin came to Mae's side.

"He gonna die?" Colin asked.

Austin reared up, instantly regretting the sudden movement. "I am not."

"He needs more than I can give him, but I trust God to provide that."

Austin eased back. "Help will be along."

Rosie knelt very close, studying him intently.

He met her gaze, holding back his pain and confusion so he wouldn't frighten her. "I'm going to be all right."

She nodded. "You promise?"

Mae's sharply indrawn breath warned him not to make promises he couldn't keep.

"You know that God is the one to decide who lives and who dies. But I certainly plan to get better and when I do, I'll take you on a picnic."

"Me too?" Colin asked.

"All of you." He turned his gaze to Mae. "All of you," he whispered.

"Children, leave him alone. He's tired."

Austin wanted to protest. Tell her to let the children stay. Their presence comforted him. But he fought to stay alert. He rested his head back and closed his eyes. The sound of Mae murmuring to the children and their quiet footsteps seemed to come from a very far distance.

"Someone's coming!" Colin's shrill call jerked Austin to alertness. Where was his gun? Then he remembered Mae taking it from him.

"Mae, my gun."

"You don't need it." Her calm voice aggravated him.

"It could be those robbers."

"You're in no condition to use a gun."

He staggered to his feet. It was all he could do not to sway, but he had to convince her he was able to stand and protect her. "My gun please." He meant to sound firm, but he heard his voice shake.

She ignored him and stood by the trail, the children at her side.

Did she think robbers would think twice before hurting a woman with children? Not the kind of men he'd encountered.

He forced his legs into stiffness. He would go to her side and protect them somehow, even if it meant standing between them and a bullet. He lifted one foot and with a jarring thud, the ground came up to meet him.

MAE LOOKED down the trail toward the approaching riders. Who would have guessed when she left Fort Macleod yesterday that she wasn't setting out on an ordinary journey to her new teaching job?

Please, God, let this be help and not more bad news. She prayed the same words over and over as she waited for the riders to draw near. She held Colin's hand on one side and Rosie's on the other. It had crossed her mind to have them hide in the trees, but the idea of standing alone to face the riders left her shaking.

"If I tell you to run, you do so immediately. Hide somewhere. And stay hidden until I say otherwise." She continued to study the approaching horsemen. Cowboy hats on their heads. Ropes on their saddles. They looked like ordinary cowboys, but she wasn't about to believe first impressions.

"What about Austin?" Rosie asked. "Who is going to look after him?"

"I will." She had no idea what lay ahead, but she would do her very best to make sure he was taken care of.

I wish things had turned out differently, he'd said.

What did he mean? Did he wish he hadn't been shot? Well, obviously. Did he wish he hadn't been the one to come upon the stagecoach where he discovered her—someone he likely didn't care to see again? Or did he wish he hadn't ridden from her life without once looking back?

She sighed. Why was she even thinking like that? There was no going back. Too much had happened in the time since he left.

A thud behind her distracted her. She glanced over her shoulder. "Austin!" He was laying on the ground.

He groaned. "That hurt."

"Can you get back to the tree?" She didn't want to leave her post.

"Sure. Of course." He half righted himself, half staggered, half crawled back to the tree and sat down. Sweat beaded his brow. He swiped his arm across his forehead.

"Rosie, sit beside him. You too, Colin." She'd face the riders alone.

The pound of approaching horses drew her attention to the trail.

Three men reined in before her and studied the situation.

"Ma'am?" They each touched the brim of their hat and nodded. They introduced themselves. Their names meant nothing and she was so intent on studying them that she forgot them as soon as they gave them.

"The stagecoach is overdue. We're looking for it. Have you seen anything of it?"

"We were on it. It was robbed by four men. The driver and shotgun rider are dead. It's back there." She pointed in that direction.

"Ah, that explains why you're here. Your husband's injured."

"He's not—" What difference did it make? "He's been shot and I fear the wound is infected. We need a wagon."

"Where are you headed?"

She explained she was on her way to the Circle A Ranch.

"It's the closest place. One of us will go and get a wagon." She remembered he'd said his name was Jones. He seemed to be the leader and waved one of the riders off. To the other, he said, "Go to the stagecoach and see what's needed." Then he swung from his horse. "Do you mind if I have a look at him?"

"I'd be grateful."

Jones knelt at Austin's side, lifted the dressing Mae had pressed to the wound. "It's infected. I've got some whiskey that will help." He reached into his saddlebag and drew out a bottle. Pulled out the cork and poured the liquid on the wound.

Mae grimaced, knowing it must hurt like fury.

Austin gritted his teeth so hard Mae could hear them creak.

The children sat back, wide-eyed and slack-jawed.

Jones held the bottle toward Austin. "This might help."

Austin shook his head.

Mae recalled he'd once told her he'd sworn to abstain from alcohol. Said he'd seen too many men and families destroyed by the stuff. He'd never given any more explanation, but she thought his father might have been addicted to strong drink.

"You sure?" Jones asked. And when Austin shook his head again, he tipped the bottle up and drank several swallows.

Mae signaled the children to her side, not wanting

them to be around a man who was drinking, but Jones corked the bottle and returned it to his saddlebag.

He looked around. "Guess there ain't much I can do until the wagon comes back. Think I'll ride around and see what I can see." He mounted up and rode down the trail.

Mae and the children released gusts of air at the same time. She chuckled. "Guess we made him as nervous as he made us." She eyed Austin, who looked a little green about the gills. There seemed little else she could do until the wagon returned and she sat near to him, the children close by, watching him anxiously.

She must do something to ease their worries. "Austin, can I get food from your supplies?"

He nodded.

She went to the horses and opened the pack where she'd seen him get food. There were sacks of dry goods—beans, cornmeal, oatmeal, sugar. He had some canned supplies. She wanted something easy to prepare and dug deeper. She found a half-round of cheese. But she had nothing to cut a slice from it. She was about to give up when she discovered a sack of hard, dry squares of biscuits. She knew exactly what it was. "Hardtack."

The children wrinkled their noses.

She chuckled. "Do you remember the lesson I taught on it?"

Rosie, ever eager to please, answered. "You said if it

was properly stored it would last forever. It was part of the rations during the American Civil War."

"That's right." She'd made some for the class to enjoy. "It tasted quite good when soaked in beef broth."

"We don't have any broth," Colin bemoaned the fact. "Nothin' but water."

"Then we'll soak some in water." She proceeded to do so. Knowing it would take several minutes for the biscuits to soften, she returned to the supplies where she'd seen the container of syrup. She pried open the tin, dipped out a spoonful and added it to the mixture.

She stirred it, breaking up the biscuits. The children watched with interest. "It's not soft yet." She continued to work at the biscuits. Several times she glanced at Austin. He sat with his head tipped back. Mostly, his eyes were closed, but once when she glanced at him, his eyes were open, watching her. It felt like he clung to her gaze; as if trusting her to get him the help he needed.

Then he closed his eyes, freeing her from his stare and from his expectations.

She vowed she would not leave him until he was safely in the care of someone who could help him.

The hardtack had softened. She gave spoons to the children and they cautiously tasted the 'pudding' she'd created.

"Good," Colin said.

Rosie rolled her eyes. "You like anything. But it's not bad."

Mae decided it wasn't the worst thing she'd ever eaten, but it certainly wasn't the best either.

The pudding was gone. The dish was wiped clean with a tiny bit of water when they saw dust in the distance, signaling the approach of a wagon.

Mae cleaned up the area, brought the horses forward and then waited, the children bouncing eagerly at her side.

Austin hadn't stirred.

She knelt at his side and touched his forehead. Hot. She resisted the urge to gently stroke his brow, but she allowed herself to murmur comfort to him. "Help is almost here. We'll get you to a place where your wound can be taken care of. You're big and tough. You'll soon be fine."

He caught her hand. "Thank you for helping me. You didn't have to."

"Surely you know me well enough to know I couldn't leave you lying in the dirt."

"I wouldn't blame you if you did."

What an odd thing to say, but then his brain was probably befuddled.

The wagon drew up to them and two men jumped down. Jones rode in at the same time.

"Austin Wagoner, I didn't expect to see you again."

Austin looked up. "Sam Thomas. Are we almost at the Circle A?"

"Almost. Sam Thomas, ma'am." The eager-faced young man took off his hat as he greeted Mae.

"Pleased to meet you. I'm Mae Martyn. This is my niece, Rosie, and my nephew, Colin." She rushed on before the man could realize she was their expected teacher. "I'm very grateful to see you. Mr. Wagoner is hurt." No one seemed to notice that she had a different last name than Austin.

"Let's get him in the wagon." Sam and the others helped Austin to his feet and practically lifted him into the back.

"Ma'am, you can ride on the bench." He glanced from the children to the horses and back to the wagon.

"The children can ride in the back too." She would feel safer to have them nearby and not on horseback.

A few minutes later they were on their way, Jones and the other man on Austin's horse, leading the packhorse.

Austin would soon be in capable hands. And she could stop worrying about him.

And she would soon be confronted with judgment for something she couldn't help.

7

"That's the ranch." Sam pointed out the buildings in the distance.

Mae saw a rambling two-story house with a wrap-around veranda, a large barn, a row of outbuildings and several smaller homes. Her employers had told her that five of the young men had married and built homes close to each other. The sixth lived a short distance away. Close enough for the children to walk to classes. Her heart opened up with a yawning ache. The ranch buildings looked nice. Tidy and welcoming. A place where she could settle in for a long spell.

Oh, if only it could be so.

The children crowded to Mae's back, anxious to see what they thought would be their new home. Mae hadn't warned them that might not be the case. The future was supposed to be secure, but instead, it opened up like a bottomless pit.

What time I am afraid, I will trust in thee. In God I will praise his word, in God I have put my trust; I will not fear what flesh can do unto me.

It was easy to trust a God she knew loved her and knew her future. Much harder not to fear what man of flesh would do to her. Think of her. Say of her.

They rattled across a bridge, passed the barn and corrals, and stopped before the house.

An older woman, knowing an injured man was coming, came from the house and hurried to the back of the wagon. That would be Mrs. Arbuckle, who'd already instructed Mae to call her Maude. "Bring him in here." She saw Mae and the children. "I believe you are the new teacher we're expecting. Come in and make yourselves at home while I take care of this man."

Sam helped her to the ground and lifted the children down, then turned to help Austin.

Mae hid a little smile as Austin insisted he could do it on his own. Thankfully, no one believed him and ignored his protests.

She followed the entourage up the steps and indoors into a warm, roomy kitchen. A big wooden table, surrounded by chairs, a cot to one side, roomy cupboards and a big stove. And a man. She and the children stopped just inside as Maude instructed the men to take Austin to the bedroom.

"Scottie, I'll be needing a good supply of water."

"It's ready and waitin'"

Scottie, the cook. Exactly as Maude had described him.

Maude, Austin, and the two men crossed the hall and entered another room. Mae tried to ease in a deep breath, but her lungs refused to cooperate.

A man in a wheelchair entered the kitchen with a sturdy young man behind him.

She knew the one in the wheelchair was John Arbuckle. Knew of his injuries. Knew that it was because of them that Maude had hired six young men and trained them to be cowboys. Those six were now married. She'd be teaching their children.

Or that had been the plan.

"Mae Martyn?" John said.

"Yes, and you'd be John Arbuckle." She introduced the children.

"I'm Leo." The young man's voice was eager, his smile wide as the sky.

"Maude told me about you and how good you are at helping John."

"I am good, aren't I, John?"

"You are very good. I don't know what I'd do without you."

Leo beamed.

Mae turned to the other man. "You must be Scottie. I'd have known you anywhere from Maude's description."

"And what would she be sayin' 'bout me?"

"That you were the best cook this side of the Atlantic Ocean and a cowboy as well." Maude had said he was wiry and tough with a rough exterior but a heart of gold.

Scottie gave a wheezing laugh. "She's exaggeratin' of course. Now sit down and I'll rustle up some dinner."

"Don't bother on our account."

Colin shuffled his feet and looked at the floor to hold back his protest.

"If'n I know anything about young uns they's ready for their next meal. Am I right?"

Colin nodded. Rosie smiled; her eyes as eager as Colin's nod.

Mae wasn't sure what to do. Should she tell John the truth about her situation immediately or wait until Maude was present? Her attention went to the doorway through which they'd taken Austin. *Lord, God, help him to be all right.* Just because he'd left her with a broken heart didn't mean she didn't still care about his wellbeing.

She turned back to John. "There's something I need to tell you."

"It can wait until you eat and until Maude can

join us."

Mae was happy to leave it as long as she could.

A few minutes later they sat around the table with a large pot of delicious smelling soup in the middle of the table.

"I'll ask the blessing," John said. "Heavenly Father, I thank You for the many blessings You've sent our way. Especially for the safe arrival of Mae and the children. Help Maudie take care of that injured young man and bless this food to our bodies. Amen."

Mae wondered if she'd be able to swallow a single bite, knowing what lay ahead, but the beef barley soup tasted so good she forgot all else for a few minutes.

"We had hardtack," Colin said around mouthfuls. "This is lots better."

Scottie chuckled. "That a fact?"

"Aunt did her best," Rosie said. "Besides, it wasn't all that bad."

"This soup is very good." Mae had brought along food, but they'd eaten what she'd packed even before the robbery. "We didn't plan for the trip to take as long as it did, so I hadn't prepared enough food." Mae knew the men must know that they were almost a day late. And one night.

Scottie served generous slices of spice cake and passed around thick cream to pour on.

Mae refused the cream. Even the cake was almost too much. A cup of tea was set before her when the bedroom door opened and the two men exited. Maude was right on their heels.

She joined them at the table. She introduced herself and acknowledged Mae's introductions. "I know you're all anxious to know how that young man is. I got the bullet out. Cleaned up the wound as best I could. He's young and strong, so he should recover. He thought he should get up and ride away, but I persuaded him that he wasn't up to it." She chuckled. "He tried to sit up but found he didn't have the strength for even that. It will be a day or two until he does."

Mae twisted her fingers together in her lap as she waited while Maude ate her meal and a generous piece of cake with lots of thick cream. Mae's nerves grew taut as the woman took her time drinking her tea. As soon as the cup was empty, she spoke. "I need to talk to you both in private." No need for the children to hear what had to be said.

John wheeled away from the table. "Let's go to the sitting room."

Maude waved Mae forward and they followed John. The room showed signs of being used a lot. A desk with a closed ledger. Bookcases crowded with books. Mae wished she could look at the titles, but chances were she'd never get the opportunity. Several soft chairs with colorful afghans on them. All in all, a welcoming room.

Mae's eyes felt heavy at the corners as she knew the welcome mat would not be extended to her.

John parked near a green armchair and turned to face Mae.

Maude sat beside him in the chair. "Please sit," she said, indicating a matching chair at an angle to hers.

Mae perched on the edge and twisted her fingers together in her lap. "I'm sure you realize myself and the children were forced to spend the night outdoors." She swallowed hard and rushed on, her voice creaking from her throat. "Austin was with us. I was very glad for his protection, but I know others will see my situation as inappropriate."

John and Maude glanced at each other.

"In what way?" he asked.

Mae's eyes stung. Were they really going to make her spell it out? "A young unmarried woman should not be alone overnight with a man and especially not one who has the task of teaching children." There. She'd said it.

"Was your behavior inappropriate?" Maude asked gently.

Mae's cheeks burned. "Of course not." She knew actions and truth didn't make people view her differently.

Maude nodded. "That's good enough for us. Seems to me you were in a situation not of your choosing.

You did what was necessary. We see no problem with that."

"You mean you'll let me teach here?" She couldn't keep the surprise and disbelief from her voice.

"We still need a teacher, and it looks like you need a place for yourself and those children you're raising, so yes, we'd be happy to have you accept the position."

The warmth of Maude's words and the way John patted Mae's hand were her undoing.

She sniffed back tears and dabbed at her cheeks with her lace-trimmed handkerchief. "Thank you. You'll never know how much I appreciate your kindness."

"I hope you'll be very happy here. Now, why don't I show you the schoolhouse and your quarters."

Mae followed Maude from the room, the children at her side, their faces anxious. "We're going to see our new home."

Maude escorted Mae and the children from the house. They walked along a dusty, well-worn path toward the row of little houses. Someone looked from one window and waved.

Maude waved back. "That's Yvette. Do you recall I told you how she and Sam rescued two little boys?"

It was the story Austin had told. "I remember. Gil and Tad. Tad is a little younger than Colin. Colin is anxious to have playmates his age." She didn't add that Rosie had complained that there were mostly boys and the only girl was seven, three years younger than Rosie.

"It's a real pleasure to have so many children surrounding us." They passed the cabins.

Behind them, on a slight rise, stood a schoolhouse so new Mae could smell the lumber.

Maude led them through a cloakroom into the schoolroom itself. The stove was cold, and a chill hung in the air, but it felt so right to be standing among familiar things. There were desks in rows, windows filled the sides, a new blackboard behind the teacher's desk and plenty of books.

Mae breathed in deeply, feeling like she'd found where she belonged. "It looks very good," she said. "I can't wait to start teaching."

"Come and see where you'll live." They passed the teacher's desk and went out through the door by the blackboard.

She stood in a room that was perfect for her and the children. The air was warm and welcoming, heat radiating from the stove. A kitchen area was on one side close to the stove with a table, chairs, and cupboards. A living area to the other side with a cot, two armchairs, and shelves she couldn't wait to fill with her books.

Thinking of the rain the previous day, she wondered if her books would still be useable. Following the advice of the older man who lived near the school at her previous position, she'd lined the crate with canvas, so there was hope. A door led from beside the bookcase and she looked into the little room. Two beds.

"We thought Colin could sleep on the cot and you and Rosie could share the room. Come spring, we'll add another room."

Tears of joy and gratitude stung Mae's eyes. It was so much better than she'd ever dreamed. "This is more than enough. Thank you."

The children explored the rooms.

How good it was to see the contentment on their faces.

Sam knocked on the outer door and then stepped in. "I think these are yours." He set their valises on the floor then left.

"The rest of my things were on the stagecoach."

"The men will bring them to you," Maude assured her. "Now I'll leave you to get settled." She went out through the schoolroom.

Mae hugged the children. "What do you think of our new home?"

"I like it," Colin said.

"How long can we stay?" Rosie asked.

Mae understood her caution. "I can't say, but let's enjoy it while we're here." She opened the cupboard doors. "Oh my. I didn't expect this." Dishes, pots and pans, towels. The next cupboard revealed everything she could wish for to make meals, from flour and sugar to spices and jars of canned meat and fruit and jams.

"Aunt Mae, look at this." Colin had gone out the exterior door.

She went to see what he had discovered and gasped. A supply of wood to one side and a row of hooks. On the other side, a small pantry with shelves and bins full of potatoes, carrots, turnips, and squash. She realized there was a vent behind the stove so she could open it during extreme cold to keep the vegetables from freezing. Her heart swelled up her throat at the kindness this revealed.

"I can't wait to teach. I can't wait to make a meal in our own little home." She drew the children back into the kitchen, held their hands, and swung their arms, laughing from sheer joy.

The children laughed, infected by her enthusiasm.

"Let's put our things away." She handed each of them their bag.

Colin stood motionless, his bag clutched to his chest. "Where do I put my things?"

She studied the cot where he was going to sleep. She wasn't sure about this arrangement. Would he settle early while she sat up to prepare lessons? Something caught her eye at the corner of the cot. "It's a little trunk for your things."

Colin happily arranged his clothing in the trunk.

Some of it was soiled from being on the ground, but Mae would deal with that later.

She and Rosie went to the bedroom. Mae claimed the top two drawers of the chiffonier and gave the bottom two to Rosie. She hung her dresses on the nails along one wall.

Done, they stood back, admiring their bedroom.

"The quilts are pretty," Rosie said.

"It's good of them to lend us such nice things."

A knock on the door took Mae's attention from admiring the room and she hurried to answer.

A woman stood in the doorway, a young boy on either side of her. "Sam said you were here. I'm Yvette, Sam's wife, and these are our boys, Tad and Gil. Welcome." She handed a saucepan to Mae. "I thought you might like stew for your supper."

"Thank you. Please come in." Yvette was a pretty young woman with brown hair and hazel eyes. She wore a warm woolen coat. The boys wore matching tweed coats and knitted caps.

"Only for a moment. I know you must be busy."

Mae chuckled. "Everything is so practical and charming that there is little for me to do." She introduced Rosie and Colin. The four children eyed one another warily.

"I want to welcome you and the children. We are so pleased to have a teacher."

Mae glanced at the two boys. They looked less enthusiastic.

"Your children are welcome to join the others and play with them. Any time they want to come visit is fine. You as well." Yvette pointed out her cabin and then left. A few minutes later, another knock sounded. Mae opened the door.

"Hello, I'm Grace. Married to Adam. It will take a few days to sort us all out." She handed Mae a loaf of bread, wrapped in a towel and still warm. "Welcome. You can see my home there." Grace pointed it out and left after a few minutes of visiting.

Mae put the loaf of bread on a platter in the middle of the table. "We will eat well tonight."

Another knock. Mae went to the door again.

"Hi, I'm Beth. Mike's wife. Welcome. I brought you a pie. You'll be teaching our son, Dakota. He's with Mike at the moment."

"Thank you. Goodness, all of you are really spoiling us."

Beth smiled. "Don't worry about cooking for a day or two. The others will bring food tomorrow. And then it's Sunday and we eat a big noon meal at the house. In the summer we gather for church service on the veranda, but it's getting too cold for that. I don't know where they plan to meet now."

"Why not use the schoolroom?"

"Of course. I hadn't thought of that. Likely, Maude and John have, but I'll mention it to them just in case."

Beth indicated which of the cabins was her home and then left.

Mae added the pie to the food on the table. "We are so blessed." The words caught in her throat. "God is taking good care of us."

The children roamed around the room. Restless. "You can go out and play," Mae said.

Colin was immediately putting on his warm coat, but Rosie hesitated.

"Where can we play?" she asked.

"You could ask Gil and Tad to show you around. You know where they live."

Colin headed for the door. "I'll ask. Come on, Rosie."

Rosie hung back. Mae went to her niece and hugged her. "It's scary meeting new people, but I think we are going to be very happy here. Everyone seems nice."

Rosie nodded and followed her brother outside. Mae watched from the window. Then her gaze went to the big house.

How was Austin faring? How long before he rode out of her life again without so much as a goodbye?

AUSTIN STAYED in bed for two days. Partly out of respect for Maude's orders, but also because he shook like an autumn leaf every time he tried to stand. To his mortification, he needed someone to help him make it to the outhouse.

But by Sunday, he was feeling up to moving about. And, more than that, Maude had told him about the church service that would be held at the school and he was determined to join the others. Austin would be able to see Mae and the children and assure himself they were safe and in one piece. He'd had nightmares about them. Robbers shooting them. Bears chasing them. All of them falling into a chasm. Him trying in vain to rescue them.

He'd awakened sweating and moaning. Maude said his restlessness was due to his infection, but he knew there was more to it than that. Seeing them would put some of his fears to rest.

After breakfast, he followed John, Maude, Leo, and Scottie across the yard. When had a few hundred feet ever felt like miles?

He was glad to reach the schoolhouse and climb the three steps into the warm room. Chairs circled the desks. Most of them were already filled. He had met some of the ranch residents when they helped Maude with his care. He didn't wait for introductions to the others but sank into the nearest chair, hoping no one would notice the sweat on his brow.

John wheeled to Austin's side and introduced everyone.

Now that he wasn't afraid his legs would let go, he took note of who was around him. But mostly his gaze went to Mae. The children sat at a desk at his elbow. She sat beside them in a chair.

He scrubbed his hand over Colin's head. The boy grinned at him.

He touched Rosie's cheek. Her smile was shy and welcoming at the same time.

"Nice to see you two."

He raised his gaze to Mae. "Nice to see you too. Are you settled in?"

She nodded. "I'll show you around after the service if you're interested?"

If only she knew how interested he was in every detail of her life.

John wheeled to the front, Maude at his side. She played the autoharp as they sang some hymns.

Austin missed this as much as anything in his mountain seclusion. Singing with others. Listening to someone else read from the Bible. Hearing exhortation. He drank in the music and words like a thirsty ground drank in rain.

The service ended and people drifted away with a reminder from Maude to come to the big house for dinner.

Mae waited until they had all departed. "Would you like to see the living quarters?"

"I would." He followed her through the adjoining door into a living area.

"I sleep here." Colin bounced on the cot.

"We sleep here." Rosie drew him to the bedroom door.

"It looks very nice."

Mae followed them as the children showed him the supplies in the cupboards, the entryway and the cold storage area, and the shelves full of books.

"Not one was ruined by the rain." Rosie seemed impressed by the fact. "Auntie covered them with canvas and it worked to protect them." The children pulled out various books and told him about them.

Then Colin went to the window. "Gil and Tad and Dakota are out there. Aunt Mae, can I go outside and play?"

"Of course. Rosie, you can go too. Missy is out there, she might like to play with you."

Rosie donned her coat with much less enthusiasm than Colin.

The door closed behind the pair.

Austin was alone with Mae. There were so many things he longed to say to her. But how did one apologize for killing someone's brother? He certainly didn't expect forgiveness.

"I wasn't sure you'd be up for the service. Is your

arm getting better?" she asked. "Sit at the table and I'll make some tea."

He sank to a chair, relieved to be sitting. "I've had enough staying in bed and being treated like a baby." He knew he sounded like a spoiled child and laughed. "I never realized how hard it is to be waited on."

"But your arm is healing?"

"It is." He didn't want to talk about his wound. But then the things he wanted to talk about were forbidden. "Maude says I won't be strong enough to ride for a few days. I'd argue with her, but she doesn't abide arguing." He chuckled again. "She says raising six boys taught her to be tough, but I'm guessing she was tough before that. Did you know she came west with John and together they started this ranch? She rode beside him until his accident."

"I've heard a few stories about them from the others. They are a friendly bunch. They have provided us with meals. I think the children will be very happy here."

She poured tea for them both and put some cookies on a plate. "We've had stew, a cabbage-rice dish that was very tasty. There's been fresh bread, an apple pie, and these cookies. Seems they want to impress us. And they are. We've been made to feel very welcome."

"I'm glad. No ill effects from the robbery or the

night in the open?" Did she understand he asked if she'd faced judgment over the facts?

The way her cheeks grew pink, he knew she did. "It's provided Colin with a wonderful adventure to talk about, though it seems most of the children have experienced some sort of adventure." Her face lit up and she leaned forward. "It's given me an idea for the classroom. I think I'd like them to write about their adventures and we could compile the stories into a book."

"That sounds like a fun project."

She ran her finger along the rim of her cup. "Maude says you'll be staying a while."

"I've agreed I should. But I won't be a burden to them. They're allowing me to live in the bunkhouse. I'll take care of myself. Except for when I need the dressing changed. I said I would pay for my keep by helping with chores but, as John pointed out, there are six men on the place, not counting himself, Scottie and Leo. At least one of them stays back to do chores while the rest ride out to take care of the cows. I said all of them could go. But John wouldn't consent."

Mae left off exploring the rim of her cup and looked at him, a smile lighting her eyes. "It sounds like you'll have to rest."

"I'll find something to do." John had said there might be need of another man come spring. Not that

Austin expected to be around that long. "Say, do you need any help teaching?"

She laughed. "It's a small class. I believe I can manage."

"No one needs me."

She sobered. "Is that important to you?"

He drank deeply of his tea. His words had been meant as a joke. But he recognized the truth in them. In the past, he'd been wanted for his gun. But that was not enough. It had never been enough. And the gun had cost him the one person who had seemed to value him as a person. "My friends at the cabin are probably wondering what's become of me."

"The wooden friends? Or the birds and skunks?"

"Yes. Though the skunks might be bedded down for the winter."

She looked out the window. "It sounds lonely to me."

He didn't have an answer. At least not one that he was willing to give. It *was* lonely. Some days he went out, no matter the weather, just to escape his own company. But what choice did he have? He'd gone to the mountain retreat to escape his reputation as a gunman. He didn't want to live by his gun. He'd stay here if he could, but he couldn't hope to spend any more time with Mae. She'd been kind because of the necessity of working together to get to safety and then because he needed help. He drained his cup and pushed back. "Thanks for the tea and the visit. I'm glad you've found a nice place."

At that moment, the clanging that indicated meal time sounded.

"I'll go with you," Mae said, reaching for her coat.

His determination of a few minutes ago to forget about enjoying her company fled and Austin smiled to himself. How many times had he wished to hear those words? Always knowing it wasn't possible. His smile flattened, replaced by a tightness in his chest that had been there for five years. As familiar to him as his own heartbeat.

A man had to accept reality. He'd enjoyed a couple of days with her. He might see a bit more of her as he recuperated. But he knew better than to hope for more.

They crossed the yard to the big house, joining the others going the same direction.

The table Austin had seen in his days at the house had been transformed. It stretched from wall to wall.

A smaller table stood nearby.

Couples found chairs and sat side by side.

"The children are at this table," Maude said, guiding Rosie and Colin in that direction. Colin seemed eager to meet the others, but Rosie hung back.

Mae bent over and whispered something in her ear. Rosie nodded and sat beside the only other girl —Missy.

He and Mae turned to the adult table. There were only two chairs left. Side by side.

Austin didn't object, but he wondered if Mae did. Though she was far too polite to say anything.

He held the chair for her, just as Ma had taught him. She smiled and murmured thanks as he sat next to her.

John looked around the gathering. "This is wonderful. Like a dream come true for Maudie and me. When Eddie died, we thought our dream had died too." He cleared his throat. "But God has more than restored to us what we lost. We are indeed blessed by each one of you." His gaze circled the table, meeting each pair of eyes. "We are especially blessed to have each of you children." He rolled to the table where the children sat with Maude at his side and they touched each of the children on their head and murmured, "You are a blessing."

Austin heard sniffing from many of those at the table. His own throat had grown so tight he couldn't swallow. It comforted him to know that Mae and the children had found a place where they would be cherished. If he couldn't be there to give them what he thought they needed and deserved, he believed Maude and John would provide it.

John and Maude returned to the table.

"I'll ask the blessing," John said and bowed his head.

Every head bowed and a holy hush filled the room.

"Heavenly Father, full of love and mercy, I thank You for these many, many blessings. For the safe arrival of our new teacher. For Austin's shoulder healing. For Rosie and Colin—two beautiful children. For each one around these tables. For the bounty of Your provisions revealed in the food we are about to eat. In the name of Your Son, Jesus. Amen."

Maude and Scottie and Grace brought the food to the table.

Austin gaped at the bounty.

John noticed his surprise and chuckled. "It must look like an overabundance compared to what a lone person is used to."

A twitch shook Mae's arm. Why? What was she thinking?

Or did he really want to know?

He'd spent years imagining what she thought, how she managed, what she did. It was good to see how she'd gone ahead with her life, following her dream to be a teacher.

That was enough for him.

8

In Mae's opinion, the first few days of teaching had gone well. The children had varying degrees of abilities, but she managed to get them enthused about a few programs.

Writing their stories appealed to the girls and Tad. But when she suggested the book of their compiled adventures would make a Christmas gift for John and Maude, whom the children called Gramma and Gramps, enthusiasm grew.

There was mixed reaction to her suggestion that they prepare a Christmas program. It was six weeks away, so they had plenty of time. She said they could choose what they'd like to do. That idea appealed to most of them.

Colin struggled to read. She'd tried everything she could to help him, but her efforts often led to him getting angry. He'd taken to visiting Austin in the bunkhouse after school and always returned in a better frame of mind.

She wondered what Austin said or did to make Colin feel better. Her curiosity provided a perfect excuse to pay him a visit.

It took a few minutes for him to answer her knock and she heard some scurrying around.

"I shouldn't have come," she said when he opened the door. "I am obviously disturbing you."

He brushed his pant legs. "Just tidying up. Didn't want you to think I'm a slob."

"As I recall—" She stopped. He wouldn't want to hear that she remembered him being neat.

"Come on in." He stepped back and she entered a large dining area. A long wooden table with benches along each side. A big stove that belted out heat. Lots of cupboards. Through the open doorway, she saw rows of bunk beds.

"Wow. This is set up to take care of a crew."

"Maude said they used to have a bunch of cowboys, but they left when John was injured."

"She told me that too."

"Now they only have extras a couple times a year. Here. Here." He grabbed a chair and drew it forward. "Sit awhile."

It seemed easier to sit than to stand and talk to him.

"Can I make you tea or something?"

Her intention hadn't been to have a social visit. Or had it? But curiosity demanded she see what he'd serve her. "That would be fine."

He went to the stove, shook the kettle then pulled it forward. He got a brown tea pot from the cupboard, rinsed it with hot water, measured in tea leaves, then poured in the steaming water. He carried the pot to the table and set it on a hot pad and then put cookies on a saucer.

"Cookies?" As soon as she said the word she remembered he'd told them he baked. "I know you said you made them, but to see the proof is surprising."

"Taste one and tell me if it passes inspection."

"I didn't mean to suggest otherwise. Of course, living alone for three years…" She paused to give him a chance to say something about why he'd chosen to do so, but he went to the cupboard for two heavy mugs and seemed not to notice. "I suppose you'd get lots of practice."

"I sure did. I guess that's why the crows like me. They got my failures." He poured tea and held out the saucer of cookies to her.

She took one and bit in. "These are delicious." Soft molasses cookies with a hint of cinnamon.

He gave a snort of laughter. "You don't have to be so surprised."

"Well, I am. Maybe you could teach me how to make these."

He lifted one shoulder. "Maybe."

They sipped tea and chewed cookies.

"I suppose you're wondering why I've come here?"

"I thought you missed me." He smiled, but his eyes were watchful.

She wondered what he really thought. Or perhaps she wondered what he was hiding. If only he would explain why he'd left her. But that was water under the bridge as they said. And the water would likely be long gone to the ocean by now. "I'm wondering how Colin is when he comes to visit you. He's often cranky after school, but he's cheerful when he comes back from here. Maybe you can tell me what you're doing that changes him."

Austin pushed his mug aside. "He's struggling to read."

Mae nodded. "I've tried to help him."

"I'm afraid I don't know how to help him read, but I can help him find other things to do that make him feel better about himself."

"Like what?" She tried not to sound annoyed. Not to be annoyed. But he made it seem like she was failing in her raising of her nephew.

"Mae, you're doing an excellent job with the children."

He'd always been able to read her thoughts, but it surprised her that he still had the ability.

"But you're his parent as well as his teacher. All I'm doing is giving him someone who isn't either. Do you object?"

"I suppose it makes me feel inadequate when he has to go to someone else for what he needs, but I can hardly object when he returns a much happier boy. What exactly do you do?"

He reached to the bench next to the wall and lifted a game of checkers. "This is one of the things we do. He's very good at the game."

Mae looked at the game board as emotions roiled through her. Too many times she'd wondered what it would be like to have Austin helping her raise the children. Her heart burned with impossible dreams. Not only for herself but for the children. "I know they need a father figure. I hope they'll find that here." Then realizing he might think she meant with him, she quickly added, "The men on the ranch are the sort of men I want the children to look up to."

His expression closed up. She couldn't tell what he was thinking. Perhaps it was a mercy. He likely had leaving on his mind.

"I promised you and the children a picnic."

She wanted to say she didn't expect him to keep that promise, but she couldn't deny herself an outing with him. "Isn't it too cold for eating outside?"

He chuckled. "It's never too cold. One just has to prepare for it. You dress warmly, build a big fire and roast food over the coals."

She couldn't help but be intrigued.

Seeing her interest, he said, "Shall we plan on Saturday unless the temperature drops drastically or there's a storm?"

"That sounds fine."

"Now tell me how school is going."

She told of the lessons. The ones that were met with enthusiasm and the ones that weren't. He chuckled as she relayed some of the reactions. When she mentioned Christmas she wondered at the way his face closed up again. Perhaps he was wishing he wouldn't be spending the season alone except for his wooden friends.

She was about to suggest he should consider spending Christmas with those at the ranch when Colin dashed into the house. Seeing Mae, he skidded to a halt, disappointment on his face.

"I was just leaving. Austin, thanks for the tea and cookies." She grinned at Colin. "Don't worry, I left some for you." She patted Colin's shoulder as she passed.

It was a good thing the boy had come when he did and saved her from making a fool of herself and embarrassing Austin with her suggestion.

And if she hurried home and dashed away tears as she went into her house, it was only because…

Because of the loneliness that accompanied every hour of her day since Austin had ridden out of her life.

Austin drummed his fingers on the table top as he watched out the window. He'd seen the children leave the schoolroom and return to their homes. He'd watched Colin run over to join Tad in some sort of game that seemed to involve hitting a stone with a stick and chasing after it. Dakota hovered nearby until Colin waved him forward to join them.

For some reason, that action filled Austin with pride. Colin was a good boy. Thanks to Mae. Since he arrived at the ranch, his prayers had been for Mae and the children to be safe. He prayed Colin would not turn out like his father. Austin had never really cared for the elder Colin, but overlooked some of his behavior because he was Mae's brother and guardian and she loved him.

"He's given me a home," she'd said several times. "And he's very kind and generous to me. Without him, I don't know where I'd be." She had grown thoughtful. "At fourteen, I'd probably have had to find a way to support myself. Maybe be a nanny or work in a hotel."

She'd shuddered then. Seems she'd given the situation some thought.

He was grateful her brother had given her a home. But there was something about Colin Senior that bothered Austin. And it wasn't only the snide comments about how fast Austin was with the gun.

He shook his head and brought his attention back to the scene out the window. The children had all gone indoors.

A lamp brightened the window in Mae's kitchen.

Austin continued to sit at the table, dusk gathering outside as well as in. He dropped his chair to all fours and leaned closer to the glass. He smiled. Then grabbed his coat and hurried out the door.

He trotted across the yard to Mae's home and rapped on the door.

Mae opened to him, surprise and curiosity on her face.

"You have to see this." He glanced over her shoulder. "All of you. Get your coats."

"What is it?"

He caught the note of caution in her voice and yet she donned her coat and followed him. He told himself it didn't mean there still existed a measure of trust between them.

The four of them stepped into the yard. He stopped. "You don't often see snow like this." Large flakes drifted down without a hint of wind. No hard, driving pellets or wet blasts.

Mae tipped her face to the snow, closed her eyes, and let the flakes kiss her skin.

The children stuck out their tongues and caught flakes.

The fading light caught and gathered in each floating crystal.

Austin watched them without appearing to stare. This was a memory that would fill many lonely hours back in his cabin.

One of the others must have noticed the snow and alerted everyone. Or perhaps everyone had noticed. The yard was soon full of children lifting their faces to the sky. Young women standing still, simply enjoying the event.

Red-headed Eva laughed and twirled. She caught Yvette's hand and they twirled together.

Grace, Beth, and Abby reached hands for each other and danced in the falling snow.

Not paying heed to his mental warnings, Austin took Mae's hands, ignoring her hesitation. He leaned back and swung her in a gentle circle. His shoulder reminded him of his recent injury, but he didn't let it deter him.

Her laugh was his reward.

From the big house came a sound. They all stopped and turned toward it.

Leo stood in front of the house, his arms raised over his head. He laughed in great gulping shouts.

They watched him for a moment.

His enjoyment and amusement were contagious and Austin chuckled. The others laughed softly as they watched him.

He began to spin around. The children followed his example.

Leo grew dizzy, staggered, and sank to the ground, still laughing.

Austin realized that he and Mae still held hands. She didn't seem to notice and he wasn't about to release her hand until she did. Why was she allowing it? Why wasn't she pushing him away, distancing herself, refusing to let the children talk to him?

She pulled her hand away.

"How's your arm?"

That was the reason. She was too kind and generous to push him away when he was injured.

"It's healing well." He blinked. Let people think it was because of the snowflakes landing on his lashes. But it was memories tugging at them. His heart ached with longing, regret, and wishes that they could return to a sweeter, more innocent time when holding hands was mutually enjoyable. When they reached for each other at every opportunity.

He remembered a time at church. They'd been sitting side by side under the watchful eye of her brother and sister-in-law. It would have been inappropriate to hold hands in church, but they'd pressed their fingers together under the guise of sharing a hymnal.

The ache inside him rose up his throat, pressed against his ribs and threatened to overwhelm him.

He'd lost it all because of his gun.

He spun away, went into the bunkhouse and found his gun belt. He took a shovel from the barn, went behind the building and started to dig.

The others had returned to their homes, so no one was aware of what he did.

The hole was big enough and he straightened.

"What are you doing?" Mae's voice came from the shadows.

"Digging a hole."

"For what purpose?" Her words were soft; as if she sensed the despair clawing at him.

He picked up his gun and gun belt and dropped them into the hole. "I am done with being a gunman."

"Austin! What if you need to protect yourself? Or hunt?"

"I have my rifle." He shoveled dirt into the hole until it was filled.

Mae still stood there. Would she see this as his remorse over having to use his gun, especially when it caused the death of her brother?

He stopped a few inches from her. "I regret ever

picking up a gun. I regret having used it to hurt another." He left her and returned to the bunkhouse, but he watched from the window until he saw her go into her house.

Then he sank to a chair and buried his face in his hands. As soon as his shoulder was healed enough it wasn't a concern, he needed to get back to his cabin. Seeing Mae every day was slowly unraveling the protection he had woven around his heart.

But the thought of never seeing her again hurt a thousand times more than any gunshot wound. He sat up, forcing steel into his heart.

He'd enjoy the picnic he'd promised them. He'd fill his mind with images of them, bury every word in his thoughts to enjoy over and over again.

But he could expect nothing more from Mae than her sweet kindness. So what if he dreamed of past kisses, felt the warmth of her hand in his from past occasions? She could not be part of his future.

And without her, his future was bleak and cold.

9

Mae enjoyed being in the classroom, enjoyed taking care of Colin and Rosie, making their meals, and listening to their chatter. They'd established a routine. But several times she found herself at the window, staring toward the bunkhouse. Occasionally, she observed Austin heading toward the barn or Maude going to the bunkhouse to tend Austin's dressing.

She thought of inviting him to join them for a meal but decided against it. To do so would only increase the dimensions of the hollowness within her. Though she could ask him about Colin again. But what more could he say?

It seemed the week would never end.

Finally, Friday arrived and with it an excuse to visit Austin.

She went to the bunkhouse. He opened the door before she even knocked. As if he'd been watching her. Waiting for her?

Don't be silly.

She stepped inside. The aroma of yeasty bread filled the room. Three golden loaves cooled on the table. She eyed them.

"What should I prepare for the picnic tomorrow?"

"I've got everything ready. It's my treat. Besides, I have nothing else to do."

"Are you sure?"

"Yup. Would you like to sample the bread?"

"It smells good enough to eat." She couldn't tear her gaze from the loaves.

He laughed. "I believe it is." He sliced off the crusty heel. He put it on a plate and handed it to her, along with a dish of butter and another of syrup.

She prepared the piece of bread and bit into it. "Umm. This is good. Austin, you could run a bakery."

He quirked his eyebrows. "I don't think you could eat enough to make a business profitable."

"But dozens of others could." Even as she spoke the words, she realized those at the ranch did their own baking. "Never mind. It was meant as a compliment."

"Thanks."

Silence followed his word. There was a time they didn't need to fill silences, content simply to be with each other. Oh, how young and foolish she'd been. But what she wouldn't do to recapture that feeling.

"Why the sigh?" Austin said.

She hadn't realized she'd sighed. "Guess it's relief to have the weekend ahead of me and be able to devote time to the children." And spend time with him.

"It must be hard being a parent on your own and having to teach as well."

His sympathetic tone touched a wound she'd tried to ignore. She wished she had time to bake cookies or fresh bread for the children to enjoy when they returned from school. "It's a challenge. But now that the children are older, it's not quite so hard."

"How did you manage when they were little?"

If only he'd shown some interest back then. "After their mother died, I had to move into a smaller place. There was a little money that carried us through until I got a job. Colin was too young to go to school, so I hired a girl. Annie was good with him and kept the place clean. But then we moved." She shrugged. "It's not always easy to find someone."

"It sounds like you've had it hard. I'm glad you found this place." He glanced out the window as if uncomfortable looking in her direction. What did she expect? He'd been unwilling to stand by her five years ago. Why would things be different now?

She pushed to her feet. "If you're sure there's

nothing I can do to help, I'll be on my way." She paused at the door. "Thank you for the bread."

"Shall we leave about ten for our picnic?"

"We'll be ready." She closed the door behind her.

SATURDAY MORNING DAWNED bright and clear. The children bounced on excited feet, hardly able to wait for the picnic. She let them put on their warm outer clothing and wait on the doorstep for Austin. They gave her details as to his progress. Not that she needed the children to inform her. Her frequent glances out the window kept her abreast of his activity.

"He's going to the barn."

"He's hitching up horses."

"Where do you think we're going?" Colin directed his question to Rosie.

"I don't care where we go. I know we'll have fun."

Mae couldn't have agreed more. She'd promised herself she would enjoy this one outing with Austin and then pull her emotions back. Stop wishing for what she couldn't have. Even stop reliving the sweet times they'd enjoyed five years ago. At least she'd enjoyed them. In hindsight, she wondered if he had or if she'd only superimposed her emotions on him.

"He's coming toward us. Come on, Auntie Mae, let's go."

Mae had only to slip into her warmest coat. She

already wore several layers of clothing and had her warmest mittens ready to put on.

She stepped outside and pulled the door closed.

Austin had stopped the wagon and lifted the children into the back. They peered over the side of the box, grinning widely.

He held out his hand and escorted her to the wagon. Her throat closed off, tears burned the back of her eyes as she recalled other times he'd done the same. Such a gentleman.

He assisted her up to the seat and then sat beside her and flicked the reins.

They were on their way. And she didn't care where they went.

The children were a little more curious. They leaned over his shoulders.

"Where we goin'?" Colin asked.

"I heard there is a very nice spot down by the river."

"How long 'til we get there?" Colin rocked back and forth in excitement.

"What's your hurry?" Austin asked. "Sometimes the journey is part of the enjoyment." He glanced over his shoulder. "You know something your aunt and I used to do?"

Two pairs of eyes widened. And two heads rocked back and forth.

"We sang." And just like that, as if five years didn't

separate them, he smiled at Mae and began singing, "'Joy to the world. The Lord is come.' Sing with me."

She joined in and then the children did as well.

Tears streamed silently down her cheeks as memories clenched around her heart.

"Mae!" He reined in. "What's wrong?"

She shook her head. The children watched, concern filling their faces. She made it a practice to never cry in front of them. She sniffed and swiped at her eyes. "Christmas always pulls at my emotions." Looking around for something to divert them, she saw exactly what she needed. "Look at those ravens squabbling in trees." Her ploy worked and the children laughed at the birds.

Austin wasn't so easily distracted. He watched her, his eyes full of concern.

She held his gaze a moment, refusing to blink or let him see the turmoil within her heart.

With a little nod of acceptance, he continued onward until they reached a grassy hill overlooking the stream and allowing them a view of the mountains to the west.

The children jumped from the wagon.

"Can we go explore the river?" Colin asked.

Mae would have liked to keep them with her, providing a buffer for her so she wasn't thinking of happy times spent with Austin, but she couldn't deny them their enjoyment.

"Yes, you may, but don't try the ice." There were patches of it in places.

The two of them hurried down the incline and were soon tossing rocks into the water or bouncing them off the ice.

"There's a lot of snow on the Rockies," she said, in hopes of keeping the conversation on the scenery.

He stared at the mountains, silent so long she grew a little nervous. Was he longing to return to his cabin amidst that snow? So cold and alone. She shuddered.

His shoulders sank and he began unloading things from the wagon. She went to help.

He pulled some wood toward him, then stopped without removing it.

"What were you crying about?"

She had no intention of telling him the truth…that her memories of days spent with him hurt like she'd been shot. "I told you. Christmas and Christmas memories."

He nodded and stared at the mountains again. "I understand that there are memories that can upset you. My pa was a drinker. For years, Christmas was a reason for him to celebrate by getting drunk. Beecher —my brother—"

As if she had forgotten even one detail about Austin.

"—would tell him to stop and that would end up in a fight. I often wonder if Beecher didn't take up shooting because, in his mind, every tin can, every shattered branch, was what he wanted to do to Pa."

"You never told me that before."

He shrugged and picked up an armload of wood. She noticed he didn't use his left arm much. "Why would I tell you such horrible things? I probably shouldn't have told you now. I'm sorry I did. But Pa changed. Said God got a hold of him." He dropped the wood in the spot he chose for the fire. "By then, Beecher was too fast to be ignored. He lived by the gun and died by the gun."

Austin sounded so sorrowful, she wondered why he'd followed in his brother's footsteps. Perhaps it was as he said, he was too fast to be ignored. For sure, Colin Senior had spoken of Austin's speed and skill with his gun, his tone full of envy and maybe even something else. Something almost sinister.

She shifted her thoughts to more pleasant things. "Christmas with my parents was nice. Pa read the Christmas story. Mama always made us new mittens. Though I don't remember Colin that much. I was only nine when he left home and moved west." She smiled as she thought of that part of her past. "I remember our last Christmas together though, of course, at the time, I didn't realize it was to be our last. It was just the three of us. Pa made a fire in the fireplace. He popped popcorn. We had gone to church earlier and the service was so beautiful. I was fourteen. You might think I would be indifferent, but for some reason, it hit me that year that Jesus had become a helpless baby. Maybe it was because my friend Sissy had a new baby brother that I saw how helpless He was. How He had to learn everything. To think that the God who made the universe took on human form. And He came with one goal in mind. To die on the cross for our sins." She paused a moment, overcome with emotion. "I read about a hanging. Heard people talking about it. The man had done horrible things, yet to hear how he'd writhed—" She shuddered. "And to think of Jesus choosing to die for me."

Tears streamed down her face.

Austin couldn't believe there was room for any more pain in his heart, but to see Mae crying split his heart into quivering fragments. He took off his mitten and wiped the tears from her face.

Her skin was cool. Her eyes glistening and yet watchful. As if seeking something. But he had nothing to give.

She leaned into his touch. Or was it only his imagination that made him think so? He squeezed the fingers on his other side tight to resist pulling her into his arms.

An ache bigger than the Rockies filled his insides and threatened to choke him.

She eased away. "I'm sorry for being so emotional."

He pulled his thoughts into submission and returned them to the conversation that had triggered her tears. Talk about Jesus' birth and the reason He'd come. "Don't apologize. I've had lots of time to read and think up in my cabin. And the truth of Jesus's birth and death moves me as well. I am so unworthy. Of any of the good things God sends into my life."

She studied him. "I expected to hear awe, but it sounds more like regret. Is it?"

There was no way he could explain or that she could ever understand the depth of his regret. "I better get the fire going." He shouldn't have offered to take them on this picnic. Should have excused himself by saying his shoulder still hurt. But he hadn't been able to deny himself this one outing. Something to carry with him into the future.

The cold, lonely future in his cabin.

It wouldn't be the only memory either. He and Colin had been doing a number of things together. The boy was very good with his hands and Austin had been helping him carve a little ornament for his aunt. It had started out as a horse but was now a dog. He'd enjoyed teaching Colin to play checkers and had listened to the boy tell about some of the struggles the little family faced.

It was almost enough to make Austin want to stay and take care of them all.

Then there was Rosie. She often came to visit or joined him when he went outdoors. She was quiet and thoughtful. In many ways like her aunt. Rosie talked about the things she liked. Flowers that she and Mae had planted wherever they lived.

"And then we have to leave them behind when they are just starting to do well."

She asked if he'd read the books she liked and when he said he had, she'd discussed them with him.

Above and beyond that, none of them would ever know, or guess, how many hours he spent watching the schoolhouse. Feeling rewarded when Mae came out to join the children in play. Or when she took out ashes. It was all he could do not to run over and do it for her.

The fire blazed and he brought out the blankets and the basket containing food.

"I'm going to find some logs to sit on." He headed for the nearby trees.

Mae hesitated a moment and then followed. "I'll help." The children were leaving the river and heading for the fire, so he understood she didn't need to keep an eye on them.

They found a fallen tree big enough to provide seating. He carried one end, she carried the other and they toted it back to the fire.

"When are we gonna eat?" Colin asked.

Austin looked at the position of the sun in the sky. "Son, it's early yet."

"But I'm hungry."

Rosie didn't say anything, but she rocked back and forth and her look said she was hungry too.

Austin looked at Mae. "What do you think? Should we let them eat this early?" Preparing the meal would take time and would be a good way to entertain them, but he waited for Mae's opinion.

She sighed and rocked her head back and forth. "You'd think I never fed them, but be assured they ate a very hearty breakfast." She looked at the children. "You can't possibly be hungry again."

"But we are," they chorused.

She lifted her hands in resignation. "I wouldn't want them to fade away to shadows. Very well." She turned back to Austin. "Do you mind if we eat now?"

He couldn't think. Couldn't answer. The smile on her face, the warmth in her eyes felt like she'd reached out and given him a welcoming touch. It wasn't possible. He knew that. Believed it. Had acted on it for years.

"Austin?"

He snapped out of his mental wrangling. "I have to admit I'm hungry too. Let's eat." He opened the supplies he'd brought. "I have to warn you that it's going to take a good hour for our food to cook."

Colin sank into himself. Rosie looked intrigued and Mae crossed her arms as if to say she hoped he knew what he was doing.

"Tell you what. You can each have two cookies while the meal cooks."

That brought the pair to life again. Even Mae brightened up.

He passed out cookies to all of them and ate two himself. Done, he dusted crumbs from his fingers.

"Now, who's going to help me?"

"Me! Me," Colin shouted while Rosie raised her hand.

"Good. Two of you. Rosie, you find the potatoes in the basket. Colin, you run and get the rocks I brought along."

"What about me?" Mae asked as the children ran to do his bidding.

She sounded so hurt that he laughed.

"It's your turn to let someone else do the work. But tell you what. I'll heat water and make us some hot cocoa." He hung a kettle of water to heat. He stirred in the dry mixture he'd prepared ahead of time. When it was hot, he dipped out some, cooled it with milk and handed the cup to Mae.

She tasted it. "Umm. This is good." She watched him over the rim of the cup. "You never stop surprising me."

The children returned. He put the rocks to heat

then buried the potatoes under the hot stones before he met her gaze. "I don't know if that's a good thing or not."

She lifted one shoulder. "I don't know either."

The children watched them, so he said nothing more. He put meat he'd prepared at home on a spit and set Colin to turning it. A few minutes later, Rosie took a turn.

The hour passed quickly as they talked about the meal and discussed what foods they liked and didn't like. Turns out Colin didn't like green beans.

"Or basically anything green," Mae said, her voice full of patient resignation.

"I like your cookies best," Rosie said.

"Then you shall have more for dessert."

She nodded, a pleased little smile upon her lips.

Mae watched her with a considering look on her face.

Austin wondered what was going through her head, but he wouldn't ask her in front of the children. He probably wouldn't ask her at all. She'd been very gracious about not bringing up Colin Sr.'s death. He preferred to leave it that way.

He checked on the potatoes and meat. "I think it's ready. Rosie, you'll find plates and forks in the basket."

She brought them over and Austin served up the meal. He offered a quick grace and they all ate.

"I'm going to live in the mountains when I grow

up," Colin said. "And I'll cook meals like this every day." The way he looked at Austin, Austin knew he was saying he wanted to be just like him.

He didn't need to look at Mae to feel her disapproval.

"This is a fun way to eat once in a while, but it's awfully nice to sit around the table with friends and family in a warm kitchen." Austin hoped his answer would mollify Mae.

"I guess." Colin sounded far from convinced.

They finished the meat and potatoes and he gave them each a cup of hot cocoa and some cookies.

As soon as the children were done, they asked to explore in the trees.

"Help clean up first," Mae said. She gathered the plates and handed them to Rosie.

"What do I need to do?" Colin rocked back and forth, anxious to do his chore so he could leave.

"Bring another piece of wood," Mae said.

Colin ran to do so and then the pair of them ran, laughing, to the trees. Their cheerful voices carried back to Austin and Mae.

Mae looked into the bottom of her empty cup.

"Do you want more?" he asked.

"Oh, no. Thanks." She heaved a sigh.

"Something bothering you?" If only she'd say what she was thinking…feeling.

But did he really want to hear? Perhaps not. Easier

to let it hang between them, forever a barrier. He didn't expect there was any way to change the facts.

She stared into the fire. "I remember—"

At the same time, he recalled something they'd done. "I remember—"

They both stopped and looked at each other. For a moment it seemed like they were back before the bank robbery; their hearts and minds in unison.

Her eyes reflected the color of the sky. Filling him with sunshine that warmed him from the inside out. It was only his imagination, but he savored the feeling.

She lowered her gaze. Her lashes fanned out on her cheeks.

The moment was over. As fleeting as a snowflake on one's tongue. "What were you thinking?" he asked.

"That time we went with the church young people to skate on the pond."

"Me too." Memories flooded his thoughts. "Do you remember how Stan threw a big log on the fire and sparks flew everywhere?"

She grinned. "And the girls squealed. Remember how Bart wanted to play Crack the Whip? It was scary to watch. I certainly wasn't going to play."

"I played."

She sobered, her eyes full of concern. "You were the tail and went flying." She shuddered. "I forgot to breathe until you slowed to a stop." She pressed her hand to her chest as if still struggling to fill her lungs.

He studied her, and with no resistance, fell into her gaze as if they were back at that time with nothing between them but sweet accord.

She had a scarf around her neck and untied it, then put it beside her.

A zephyr of wind caught it and carried it toward the river.

He was instantly on his feet, chasing after it. She bounded after it as well. They ran down the slope.

The scarf rose and twirled just out of reach.

The wind subsided. The scarf fluttered. Austin reached for it before the wind caught it again. His gaze was on the bit of fabric so he didn't realize Mae had also lunged for it.

His fingers closed on the material at the same time as his body collided with Mae's. He caught her to keep from knocking her over, his arms closing around her. His heart pounded. His lungs struggled for air. He needed to let her go. But his arms refused to obey.

Just a few minutes of holding her, enjoying her sweetness.

She tipped her face to him. Smiling. Her eyes shining. Just like she'd looked that first time he kissed her. So sweet. So loving and giving.

He lowered his head slowly, uncertain. Was she really inviting him to kiss her?

She certainly wasn't pulling away and he gave her plenty of opportunity to do so.

With a muffled groan he caught her lips. Held them with his for a moment. The world swirled away in a breath of wind. Nothing existed but Mae and his love for her. A love that had not weakened despite their separation. Despite the reason he'd had to leave her.

She jerked away. "Austin, what were you thinking?"

Well, he'd been thinking she liked his kiss as much as he did. He eased back from her, his arms cold and empty. It seems he was mistaken.

"You can't kiss me." Her voice was husky.

"I just did." But he knew what she meant. There was too much between them. Too much to forgive or overcome. "I'm sorry. Let's get packed up and go home." Only it wasn't home for him. There was only one place where he belonged. In the mountains with his wooden friends and wild creatures.

Why had he let himself think otherwise?

What was he going to do about the way he felt?

10

Mae called the children to return. She had to get back as soon as possible. What was wrong with her that she not only let Austin kiss her, she welcomed it? Would have lingered in his arms feeling his warmth and strength. Except for the facts. He'd tired of her before. She could see no reason he wouldn't do so again. She'd never really healed from that heartbreak and couldn't imagine she'd survive another.

As if sensing her hurry, Austin moved quickly to put the fire out. He had the children carry back the rest of their supplies.

Mae allowed him to assist her to the wagon seat, even knowing it was sweet sorrow to have him touch her.

As soon as she was seated, she folded her mittened hands together and stared straight ahead.

Austin sat beside her. Studied her for a moment, but she didn't shift her gaze. With a soft sigh, he picked up the reins and turned the wagon toward the ranch.

The children must have sensed the strain between Mae and Austin. They started out leaning over the backs of the adults then sat down in the back.

Mae wanted to assure them they'd done nothing wrong. No reason they should blame themselves for the sudden change in the atmosphere.

She sucked in a deep breath then looked over her shoulder. "Did you have fun?"

Colin was on his feet and moved forward. "I saw a big nest." He held out his arms as far as they would go. "What kind of bird do you think built it?"

Austin gave the boy a soft look. "Maybe a hawk or an eagle." His gaze shifted to meet Mae's. She wished she could erase the regret and sadness in his eyes.

Sadness? Why was he sad? He was the one who'd left.

She shook off the thought and turned to Rosie, who watched the others, not yet ready to believe everything was as it should be. Not that Mae could blame her. How many times had the girl seen adults talking together and then learned they had to move again?

"Rosie, did you see anything special?"

Rosie withdrew her hand from her coat pocket. "I found this." She moved forward to reveal a cluster of rose hips. Still red, though the skin was wrinkled. "Aren't they pretty?"

"They are indeed. Why don't you put them in a little dish when we get home?"

"Did you know that rose hips are good for you?" Austin directed his attention to Rosie. In fact, it seemed to Mae that he studiously avoided looking at her.

Well, what did she expect?

"Really?" Rosie was intrigued. Maybe in part because of her name.

"Yes, they are good for pain and curing colds."

Mae stared down the trail. Too bad they weren't useful for curing a broken heart. She should never have agreed to this outing. A few minutes of pleasure would result in hours, days, weeks—never-ending pain. Though one would think she might have grown used to the pain by now.

"Aren't you going to sing again?" Colin asked.

"What would you like us to sing?" Austin asked, sounding wary.

Not that Mae could blame him. She, for one, would find it hard to sing of Christmas and good things.

"You know any fun songs?"

Grinning widely, Austin sang, "'All around the

cobbler's bench, the monkey chased the weasel. The monkey thought 'twas all in fun. Pop! Goes the weasel.'" At the pop, he flipped his palm in front of Colin, moving so fast the boy jumped and giggled.

Austin sang several verses of the song as the children laughed.

"More, more," Rosie begged when he finished.

Austin began another song. "'Buffalo gals won't you come out tonight.'"

Mae gritted her teeth and stared down the twin tracks the wagon had made earlier in the day. Had he chosen that song on purpose? But why? Did he plan to torture her with memories of their past?

The first time she'd heard the song was back at Fort Benton. A minstrel group had gathered a crowd around them down on the wharf. Hearing the music, Mae and Austin had gone there. There were several rousing songs before the performers sang the buffalo gals one. The music was certainly toe-tapping.

Austin had caught Mae's hand and the two of them tapped their feet together in a perfectly matched dance. As if they breathed the same thoughts. As if their hearts beat in unison.

Mae tried in vain to stop the rush of memories. She closed her eyes and held back the tears stinging her eyes.

They had stayed until the minstrels departed. Then, rather than return home, they wandered along the river. It had been spring and flowers bloomed everywhere. A warm, gentle breeze came off the water. Mae had never seen the land more beautiful. She readily acknowledged that her appreciation flowed from a full heart that made her see everything with such delight.

They'd sat on a grassy hill and he'd kissed her for the first time.

This afternoon's kiss reminded her of that first one. Sweet, gentle, giving. Promising. Except the promises were meaningless.

Why had he left so hurriedly? What had she done?

The words bled from her heart. From a wound that would never heal.

Thanks to Austin's efforts, it didn't seem the children wondered why she was quiet on the journey home.

The wagon stopped in front of her place. The children jumped down. Mae managed to get to the ground on her own. After all, she was used to being on her own. Doing everything a father and mother would do. And she didn't regret one thing about it. The children made it all worthwhile.

Austin stood waiting by the door.

"Children, what do you say?" she prompted.

"Thank you, it was fun." Colin's exuberance was clear.

"Thank you. I like winter picnics." Rosie blushed at her admission.

"I had fun too." Austin squeezed each of their shoulders and the children went inside.

Mae thought to slip by with a hurried, "Thank you." But Austin didn't move aside.

"Mae, I know I offended you and I'm sorry. It was not my intention."

A turmoil of emotions rushed up her throat. "Then what was your intention?" She pushed by him and closed the door firmly, but not before she heard him mutter,

"I couldn't help myself."

AUSTIN PUT AWAY the picnic supplies and took the horses to the barn, all the while trying not to think.

Pete was in the barn when Austin entered and studied him openly.

"For a man who spent the better part of the day in the company of a pretty young woman and her two wards, you look awfully down in the mouth."

"Huh," was all Austin said as he brushed one of the horses.

"Something happen?"

Guess it was too much to hope Pete would leave

him alone. That was one thing about living in the mountains. No one plagued him for explanations.

No one cared one way or the other what he did or how he felt.

That was a good thing. Wasn't it?

Pete grabbed a curry brush and worked along with Austin. "I can tell you that things don't always go smoothly when a man is courting. Take me and Eva—"

Austin straightened and gave the man a sour look. "Who's courting?" Certainly wasn't him.

Pete straightened too, facing Austin across the horse, an unrepentant grin on his face. "Some things don't need to be spelled out. They're as plain as the tail on this horse."

"News to me." He resumed currying the horse and found he had to hold back out of concern for the poor thing.

Pete chuckled. "Sometimes we're the last to know."

Austin brushed long, even strokes. Last to know. Huh. "There was a time in the past...far past...when I courted Mae." He spoke softly, not caring if Pete heard or not, but feeling a need to empty his chest of some of the bottled-up feelings. "But things didn't go very well." His hands grew still. He realized Pete had stopped brushing as well and stood at the horse's head, watching him.

"John and Maude often say that there's no broken

fence that can't be mended. They taught us to forgive others, but also ourselves."

Austin resumed brushing. "Some things are unforgivable."

"I don't agree. If God can forgive, who are we to refuse to offer it?" Pete put away his brush and left the barn.

"Guess that's all he has to say," Austin mumbled and couldn't decide if he regretted the man leaving more than he found his advice annoying.

"I don't expect her to forgive me." The words barely whispered from his lips but screamed in his head.

He finished with the horses and took an inordinate amount of time putting things away. He did not want to go to his lonely quarters.

Shouldn't he be used to being alone by now?

But he wasn't.

Finding no more reason for delay, he crossed to the bunkhouse. The fire had died down and the room was cold. Dragging his weary feet across the floor, he stirred the embers and added more wood. Soon warmth filled the room. But did not touch his heart.

He looked in the cupboards but didn't see anything he cared to prepare for his evening meal. He sat at the table. The dog Colin was carving sat on the bench, out of sight, in case Mae dropped by.

Austin put it on the table and stared at it. It was

about done. In fact, it was fine the way it was. Mae would appreciate the thought her nephew had put into the gift.

Gloom filled the room, but he didn't bother lighting a lamp. Instead, he shifted his chair so he could see the teacher's quarters. A lamp glowed on the kitchen table. A shadow crossed in front of the window. Mae. No doubt making supper for the children. In his mind, he could hear them chattering and Mae laughing at something they said. From what the children had told him, he knew she would have them help her. After supper, they would wash and dry dishes together, then read or play table games. Rosie said she had some colored pencils and liked to draw pictures.

Family living and sharing and enjoying.

An ache the size of the sky sucked at his insides.

He wanted to be part of a family—specifically that family.

What did a person do when their dreams were an impossibility?

11

Mae tossed and turned the entire night. Thankfully, Rosie slept through her aunt's turmoil. Twice Mae got from her bed and traipsed over to look out the kitchen window. Both times she was certain a light glowed in the bunkhouse. It seemed Austin was also having trouble sleeping.

He'd said he was sorry. For the kiss.

But he'd never said sorry for leaving her. Nor had he offered a word of explanation.

Would she forgive him if he did?

She'd answered that question for herself years ago. Yes, she'd forgive him. All she wanted was a reasonable explanation. One that didn't make her feel like she'd been mistaken in thinking he cared.

How many times had she tried to come up with a reason? Other than he simply got tired of her. Things such as he had a dreadful disease and didn't want her to see him suffer. But the last few days had made that excuse null and void. Or that he was already married and had forgotten about it. That was simply silly and unbelievable. Or maybe someone was trying to kill him and he had to escape. But there was no evidence of that in recent days. For one thing, he didn't look over his shoulder any more than anyone else.

He'd buried his gun. She still thought it a rash thing to do. He'd once worn it almost always. As a lawman, he had to be prepared for trouble. Sometimes, she thought wearing the gun invited trouble. Especially with his reputation of being fast on the draw.

She couldn't think what it meant that he'd buried his gun. Was he trying to tell her something? If so, she didn't understand what it was.

She wrapped her arms around her waist and stared at the flickering light across the way.

Did him kissing her give her the right to ask for an explanation?

She couldn't think of a better reason.

Finally, the light in his quarters went out and she returned to her bed. Tomorrow she would ask. Even if she didn't like his reason, it was better to know than to always wonder.

. . .

Sunday morning dawned sunny and clear. She fed the children and prepared for the church service. The rattle of chairs in the schoolroom informed her some of the men were preparing the room, but she hadn't seen Austin leave the bunkhouse. She might have missed him, but she doubted it.

When she heard women's voices, she and the children joined the others in the schoolroom.

Austin had not yet appeared. She sat close to the door so she would be able to see him, even if he came in late. The man might have overslept after being up half the night.

Everyone else had gathered and Maude began to play a hymn.

Rosie touched Mae's arm. "Where is he?" she whispered.

"I don't know." Then there was no more time for talk.

Colin's attention was on the windows that allowed him to see a corner of the bunkhouse.

Mae forced herself to concentrate on the singing and then John's words.

"How much is too much?" John asked.

That instantly had her attention.

"When is waiting too long? When is forgiveness too hard? When is not having our prayers answered too much to bear?"

She listened as he encouraged them all to trust God

for their *too much,* whatever it was. But she wondered if he shouldn't have added to trust God when enough was enough. Because she'd had enough.

Enough wondering what had driven Austin away.

Enough waiting for him to offer an explanation.

She knew what she must do and was primed to confront Austin and demand an explanation.

John was in the middle of this final prayer when Colin erupted from his seat. "He's leaving." He raced out the door.

Mae waited only long enough for John to say amen and then followed after Colin, Rosie right beside her.

Austin rode his horse, his packhorse loaded and following. She knew at a glance he was packed to go to his mountain retreat.

If Colin hadn't seen him, he would have ridden away. Again, leaving without so much as a word.

Pain gouged out her insides and robbed her of speech.

Colin caught up to Austin and grabbed his leg. "Why're you leaving? Why can't you stay?"

"I have to go." He brushed the boy's hands off and kicked the horse into a trot leaving Mae and Rosie unable to catch up.

"You can't go," Colin screamed. "I won't let you."

Mae caught Rosie's hand and they watched poor Colin begging for Austin to stay.

"Take me with you," Colin screamed again and

grabbed the packhorse. He slipped and fell under the hooves of the animal.

Mae screamed and rushed forward.

The pack animal had refused to move, forcing Austin to stop. Seeing Colin on the ground, he leaped from his saddle and rushed to the boy, scooping him up in his arms.

Mae reached them. "Colin!" Blood oozed from a cut on his cheek.

"I'm not hurt," he said. "Put me down."

Austin set him on his feet.

Colin bunched his fists. "You was gonna leave us." He turned and stomped away.

"Go with him," Mae said to Rosie.

Rosie looked from one adult to the other, then went after her brother.

"He shouldn't have run after the horse," Austin said.

Mae was shaking inside and out, but she would have her say. "You left once before without saying goodbye. Without explaining why you were leaving."

"How did you expect me to explain that I'd shot your brother?"

"Shot—" Not another sound came from her mouth. The world swirled. Lights danced before her eyes. "You shot Colin?" She could barely get the whispered words out.

He drew his hand down his face, pulling gouges around his mouth. "I thought you knew."

"I was told there was a shootout with the bank robbers and Colin was hit."

"He came gunning for me. I tried to stop him with a bullet to the shoulder." He patted his own shoulder as if she wouldn't know what he meant. "I walked away. Done with him. I didn't want to shoot him. Someone called out a warning. I turned just in time to see him aim at me. I—I—" He tipped his hands out. "I gave up carrying a gun that day. Though I've been forced to strap it on a time or two when I owed someone the favor. But never again. I've made sure of that." He swung to his saddle and rode away.

She stood there, surprised that blood didn't pool around her feet as her insides bled with shock and pain. He'd shot her brother. She'd lost them both the same day. One to death. The other to regret.

She stumbled to her home. Before she got there, Maude was at her side. "Colin, Rosie, go see Yvette and Sam. Come along, Mae, let's get you in out of the cold."

She shivered so violently she could hardly walk, but not from the cold. Maude helped her into the house and onto a chair, then put the kettle to boil

"What did you hear?" Mae asked

"I heard enough to know the man is disappointed with himself. And you have had a great shock. The others hung back so they didn't hear. It's your secret to do with as you wish."

The kettle boiled and Maude made tea.

"Do as I want? I can't even fathom the truth of what he said. He shot my brother. Then left me." She couldn't decide which pain was worse.

She sipped the tea placed before her. Absorbing the warmth into a bottomless cold cave. "Do you mind if I don't join the others for dinner today?" She couldn't think of eating or of trying to visit.

"That's fine. We'll keep the children. Give you time to sort things out."

Mae murmured her thanks as Maude left the room.

And then it was just her and her thoughts.

Austin shot her brother. If he wasn't known to be fast with his gun, Colin would still be alive. It was his fast gun that made the sheriff hire him. Guns killed people. Live by the gun. Die by the gun. Only it was her brother that died. The father of Colin and Rosie. Losing her husband had taken Betty's life too.

Live by the gun. Die by the gun.

A tooth for a tooth. An eye for an eye. A life for a life.

She downed the rest of the now-tepid tea and went to her valise. She hadn't seen that heart-shaped locket since the robbery. It must have stuck in a corner of her bag. She looked but didn't see it. Turned the bag over and shook it. Nothing fell out.

It must have gotten lost during the robbery. Good. It saved her from having to throw it out, for she wanted no memories of Austin. A gunman who'd killed her brother.

She went to the window and stared out. No need to look toward the bunkhouse. He was not there any longer. He was headed up to his mountain cabin and his wooden friends.

She slammed her hand against the window frame. Was it only a few hours ago that she had decided knowing the truth was better than wondering?

How wrong she'd been.

To know that the man she'd once loved had killed her brother burned inside like scalding water. She faced the room. Her home. Hopefully for some time. She breathed deeply. Her task was to make this work. She'd be the best mother Colin and Rosie could have. She'd be the best possible teacher.

She went into the classroom and began lesson preparations for the coming week.

HER LIFE SETTLED into a routine in the following days. She was certain no one would guess at the depth of her sorrow. She smiled at the children. She listened to their concerns and questions. She showed them how to do their tasks. If anything, she was more patient with them than before. All of these children had endured loss. It was a wonder that they were able to function as well as they did.

As they wrote their stories of adventure, she saw the depth of loss they revealed and her heart ached for the pain that accompanied their lives.

She found comfort in reading the Psalms even as she had when Austin left the first time. A fragile peace began to grow within her.

She worked hard to make her lessons as appealing as possible and was rewarded when the children eagerly took on learning their parts for the Christmas program.

Colin was a different matter. He fought reading. Argued about chores and often disappeared. She knew he went to the bunkhouse, even though there was no heat. And no Austin. She understood how betrayed he felt.

Rosie grew quiet. Retreated into reading. At bedtime one night she finally put her fears into words. She whispered to Mae, "Will he ever come back?"

"I don't think so."

"But why? What did we do?"

"You didn't do anything at all. Something happened in Austin's life that makes him sad." She'd never told the children the truth about their father's death and didn't plan to ever do so. Enough to say that he had died in an accident.

"But we could help him feel happy."

Oh, the sweet innocence of a child. "I don't know if anyone can do that for him." She couldn't even say if he wanted comfort from others.

"Doesn't he know that God can help him? Grampa John says God's mercy is new every morning. He says that means we can always start over every day."

"I don't know whether or not he knows."

"I will pray he finds out." And Rosie prayed for Austin every night.

Mae couldn't tell the child that there was so much more to it than that. Besides, wasn't it up to God to answer Rosie's prayers?

A few days later, snow fell. Not like the snow when she and Austin had held hands

For a few minutes, in the dusky stillness, she had let herself think there might exist some remnant of their feelings for each other.

This snow was wind-driven and blinding and the men were out taking care of the cows. She'd been in the west long enough to know the animals could perish in a storm. Cowboys had the difficult task of keeping them safe.

She knew the women must worry about their husbands. Despite the weather, she did not worry about Austin. He'd survived years living alone in the mountains. This snowfall was not anything new for him to deal with. Even if his gun was buried behind the bunkhouse. He still had his rifle. He'd be just fine.

So long as he was safe in his cabin. She would not allow herself to think otherwise.

The women visited her often. She knew they were trying to cheer her up. But they needn't have bothered. She was fine. Her life was good. She had the children and her teaching. She didn't want or expect more.

The weather grew increasingly cold.

"Will Austin be warm in his cabin?" Rosie asked.

Mae knew her niece's thoughts were often on him.

"He's dealt with winter before. I'm sure he's all right."

Colin looked from his sister to his aunt. His face twisted in confusion and misery and then he rushed outdoors. She understood his anger and confusion. She thought of going after him but would give him time to sort out his feelings. If he wasn't back in half an hour, she'd find him and bring him in from the cold. Not that she had to wonder where he was. He'd be in the bunkhouse where he often went.

He returned before her deadline, his arms full of wood that he dropped into the wood box.

"I'm sorry," he said.

She wasn't sure what he was sorry for, but Colin continued before she could ask.

"Austin always said I must do my best to help you. I want him to be proud of me when he comes back."

Mae opened her mouth to say Austin was gone and wouldn't be back, but she closed her mouth without saying anything. If it comforted Colin to think it could happen, why should she rob him of that? So she let it go.

In school, all the children had written their stories. What lives they'd endured in their short span of years. But now they were all part of the ranch. Part of a large, loving family.

She could want for nothing better for Colin and Rosie.

She stayed up in the evening, copying the children's stories. She would put the originals together to give to John and Maude but she meant to present a booklet to each child and hoped they would cherish the telling of the separate journeys that had brought them to this place. When she came to Rosie's story, she struggled to keep tears from falling on the page.

Rosie's story.

My name is Rosie Martyn. I am ten. I have a brother, Colin. He's eight. This is the story of my adventure. My Mama and Papa died when I was five. I hardly remember them because Aunt Mae is the only mother I remember. We lived many places because people didn't want Aunt Mae to stay and teach even though she is a very good teacher. She taught me to read and write and look how good I can write. Maybe someday I'll write real stories. We had to leave because some people didn't think Auntie could teach their children if she had her own children. See, we are her children even if we had another mama.

Mae dabbed at her eyes before she could continue.

Auntie saw an advertisement in the newspaper for a teacher at the Circle A Ranch. She read it out loud to us and we all decided it sounded like a nice adventure. We were very excited when she got the letter saying we could come. We packed up our belongings. Auntie was very smart to wrap the books in canvas so rain wouldn't ruin them. We rode the train as far as Fort Macleod then got on the stagecoach. I had never ridden in a stagecoach so I was excited. It was dusty and bounced and swayed but it was fun. Colin looked out one window and I looked out the other. Now, this is when it gets real scary. Suddenly there were men shooting. And shouting for the strongbox. Auntie says it had a lot of money in it. They shot the driver and the man beside him. I was so scared. Auntie was holding both of us tight and praying for God to help us. The horses were running real fast. A wheel snapped. I heard it but at first, I didn't know what it was. Then we were sliding down a steep hill. I was even more scared. What if we got thrown out and the stagecoach landed on us? We stopped. Both Auntie and I were afraid to move but Colin poked his head out the window and said a man had ridden up and the four robbers rode away. The man came down to help us. In case you haven't guessed, it was Austin. He helped us get here. He was shot by one of the bad men but I guess his arm must be better by now. I wish Austin hadn't left. I liked knowing he was here to help us. Grampa John says we should ask God for things we need so I'm asking God to bring Austin back. That's my adventure. Rosie.

It took Mae much longer to copy Rosie's story than the others as she had to back away many times to mop at her eyes. She didn't know how to deal with Rosie's prayer, but again she reminded herself that prayers were God's business.

But she could do her part to make Rosie happy. And Colin. She'd plan a special Christmas for them.

The next afternoon, she sent the children out to play and opened her trunk. It contained things she didn't use often or not at all, but didn't want to get rid of. Perhaps she'd forgotten and put the gold locket here. She emptied the trunk, shook every article. But she didn't find it.

She sat back on her heels and told herself she didn't want it. Didn't want the memories and lost dreams it reminded her of. But a tear trickled down her cheek. She dashed it away and carefully returned everything to the trunk and if she looked for a locket hidden somewhere amongst the items she was only being careful.

She set aside two things for Christmas gifts for the children. For Colin, his father's old cap. For Rosie, her mother's pretty hair combs.

There was a photograph of Colin Sr. and Betty on their wedding day. Mae rubbed her fingertip over the likeness of her brother. He hadn't been perfect. Had wanted things beyond his means and went after them in the wrong way, but he was her brother. And she missed him. She sniffed back tears. Then, hearing the children outside, she put everything back, closed the trunk, and shoved it into the corner. She dried her eyes and went to welcome her niece and nephew home.

The days passed in a pleasant enough routine. Mae made sure to keep busy with lesson preparations and plans for the Christmas program

There would be a break from lessons after Christmas. She wasn't sure what she'd do to occupy herself but determined she'd keep busy and do things to make the days enjoyable for the children.

Every Sunday, they gathered in the classroom for church. John always spoke encouraging words. Mae knew he must be aware of what had transpired between her and Austin, but he never said anything in his little talks that seemed directed at her. Instead, he spoke often of the gift of Jesus's birth that they celebrated at Christmas. It reminded Mae so strongly of what she'd said to Austin. How she'd been moved to tears to know God became a baby and then grew up to die on the cross.

For everyone.

For her.

John was speaking still. "Let's not forget that we

are all sinners saved by God's grace. None of us are more worthy or less worthy in His sight."

The words echoed in Mae's head through the following hours. She was no more worthy of forgiveness than Austin.

But she hadn't killed a man. She hadn't said she loved someone, then left them.

She was still a sinner, in need of God's grace.

Well, she wasn't thinking that *God* couldn't forgive Austin. Forgiveness was God's business.

But if ye forgive not men their trespasses, neither will your Father forgive your trespasses.

Lord, what You ask is too hard.

With men this is impossible, but with God all things are possible.

Her mental wrangling drove her out for a walk one afternoon. She'd asked Yvette if the children could stay with her for a few hours.

"Certainly. Take all the time you need."

She walked down to the river called Logan Creek. It was frozen except for bubbling water that made its way down the middle. She studied the running water for a moment, wishing she could be like that. Ignoring the hard things of life and singing merrily as it moved along.

However, she was not water and ice, though there seemed to be a lot of the latter around her heart. The layer had grown thicker since she learned the truth from Austin.

Could she forgive him?

Something she'd seen in her Bible reading raced through her mind. *Do not harden your hearts.*

Was that her? A hard heart of unforgiveness?

A new heart also will I give you, and a new spirit will I put within you: and I will take away the stony heart out of your flesh, and I will give you a heart of flesh. She didn't know where that verse was in the Bible, but John had mentioned it one Sunday at the dinner table. She couldn't even remember the context of him quoting it, but it was clearly meant for her on this occasion.

She sat on the cold ground to reason through her confusion. "Lord, help me understand what You want."

To forgive.

"Show me how to do that."

She thought of Colin Senior. How often he'd said something critical and harsh about Austin. Things like he thought he was better than most men because he was fast with a gun. Or he'll learn it isn't enough to be fast. Someday, someone will come along and cut that man down to size. So many times Colin had spoken like that.

As if he wished Austin was dead.

Even wished he could be the one to shoot him.

He'd tried and failed and he died as Austin defended himself.

Tears flowed down her cheeks, but she dashed them away. She'd loved her brother despite his flaws. But she couldn't blame Austin for his death.

Nor should Austin blame himself.

Lord, I forgive him. If only she could tell him so. But he'd retreated into the mountains again. For how long this time?

She understood he came out once or twice a year to get supplies. But he could go to Fort Macleod and never come near the Circle A Ranch.

Lord, would You in Your kind mercy, help Austin to accept Your forgiveness and forgive himself. And bring him here when he goes out for supplies so I can tell him I forgive him.

She stayed there until the cold seeped into her bones, then returned home, stopping to collect the children on her way.

Yvette looked at her. "I can see the time away has been good for you."

Did it really show that a load had been lifted from her heart?

Yvette continued. "Feel free to leave the children here any time. I enjoyed them and I think they enjoyed themselves."

The children carried brown cookies shaped like round little men. They chattered happily as they crossed to their home. Yvette had given them pieces of gingerbread and they'd made gingerbread men.

"Aunt Yvette told us a story about the gingerbread boy," Rosie said.

"The gingerbread boy jumped from the oven and ran away. But in the end, the fox tricked him and ate him up." Colin seemed to think that was funny.

Mae ruffled his hair. "I'm glad you had fun."

"I like it here. Except that Austin is gone." Colin bit the head off his gingerbread man.

"He'll come back," Rosie said. "I know he will. I ask God every night to bring him back."

"I hope it's soon." Colin bit off both legs. "He should have never gone."

Rosie glanced at Mae. "Auntie says he was upset about something."

Colin glowered at his aunt. "Did you do something to him?"

"I don't think so. It's something he has to work out on his own. But I think he will." Her faith clung to God's power to move mountains. Only in this case, she wanted Him to move a man off a mountain.

The days passed. Christmas drew nigh. It was time for the program to be presented.

The children had practiced their lines. Mae had finished the booklets and thought they looked very nice. They ate an early supper then she helped the children put on their best clothes. She curled Rosie's hair. Her mother's combs would have looked very nice holding back the curls, but Mae wanted to save them for Christmas.

They stepped into the classroom. The desks had been pushed together and chairs set up. There was space at the front where the children would stand.

Mae had let the children make decorations. Colored paper chains and bright hand-drawn pictures. With Mae's supervision, they had cut large letters, colored them, and hung them over the blackboard to read, 'Jesus Is Born.'

She paused as the words settled into her soul.

What love that God sent His Son to earth.

The outer door opened and the others streamed in.

Mae waited until they were all seated, then stood at the front. "Welcome."

A thud interrupted her. All eyes turned toward the sound.

12

Austin paused from shoveling snow to blow on his fingers. Even with heavy leather mittens lined with woolen ones, his hands hurt from the cold. But he had another five feet to get to the corral and little barn where his horses were and he bent to the task.

Snow, snow, and more snow. Seemed it was never-ending. He shoveled it from in front of his door. He shoveled it so he could get to the horses. He shoveled a path to the outhouse. He barely finished before he had to do it again. Had it always been like that? If it had, it felt different now.

Because of his injured arm. No other reason.

And cold. Bitter cold that squeezed his bones and encircled his heart. His breath whooshed out and froze on his face. White frost whiskers hung from his woolen knitted hat. He hadn't shaved in days and his whiskers grew white with frost.

His shoulder burned. He'd put a wet towel outside when he left his house. It would be frozen when he returned and he'd use it on his shoulder to ease the pain.

He reached the horses and paused to catch his breath. He had hay and grain for the animals, having hauled it in prior to the trip where he'd encountered Mae and the children.

Mae! He would never think of that name without an accompanying shaft of pain. He groaned, earning him a sympathetic nicker from one horse. Austin patted the animal.

The wind picked up, moaning around the corner of the enclosure. He didn't want to venture into the open again, but he couldn't stay in the barn all day. He lingered a bit longer, then patted the horses one more time, shrugged deeper into his coat, and ventured into the unwelcoming outdoors.

Already, the pathway was drifting in. He'd have to shovel again.

His world had narrowed to surviving snow and cold.

He grabbed the frozen towel, then went into his cabin. At least the fire still burned. The room was warm. Yet it felt cold. He went to the stove and shook the kettle. He could make tea. Or even coffee. He had flour and sugar, cornmeal, and oats. Numerous other dry goods and canned goods. Probably enough to manage until spring. But the thought of going out after break-up held about as much appeal as shooting himself in the foot.

He decided against making tea and went to the window. He scraped a hole in the frost so he could see out. What was there to see but snow drifted against the trees and the walls of the horse enclosure? Snow bending the boughs of the evergreens. His woodshed was almost buried in snow. His wood supply was dwindling. He'd have to venture out and find wood before winter ended.

He rubbed the glass again. There was no sign of life out there. No children playing. No teacher ringing a bell to call them in. No young women crossing from house to house. No men trotting home, eager to see their families.

No one but him. Alone.

He turned his back to the window. If he'd known Mae didn't realize he'd been the one to end Colin's life, things might have been different. He wouldn't have said what he did. They could have started over. He'd court her like she deserved to be courted.

Like he'd courted her before Colin's death.

A smile warmed his face as he recalled those sweet days.

The first time he'd seen her, she was with her brother. They stood in front of a store window, looking in. Mae had gestured at something, then turned to her brother and spoke animatedly. Then she'd laughed, the sound carrying to Austin where he'd stopped at the corner of the street to watch. Mae had hugged Colin's arm. Austin grinned as he remembered, thinking her affection was so plain she must be married to that man.

Yet, he lingered for a moment longer, watching. She made him want to find someone who could smile and laugh like that. Was openly affectionate. Then he moved on, patrolling the streets.

His new role as deputy sheriff made it necessary for him to know about everyone, so he'd asked around and discovered Mae was sister to the man he'd seen her with. He began to watch for her.

He saw her at church, but she was with her brother, his wife, and two little ones. He'd thought of slipping in beside the small family, but there wasn't room. He'd seen her again when she volunteered to help entertain the children. And had managed to help. But he never seemed to find an opportunity to make his interest known.

Then he'd seen her go into the store alone and waited outside for her to leave, lounging against the wall as if the only thing he had in mind was watching people go by.

The door beside him had opened and he'd straightened.

"Miss." He'd touched the brim of his hat.

She nodded. "Good morning."

"It is indeed."

She began walking in the direction of her home. He fell in step beside her. She glanced at him. "Can I do something for you?"

He'd given what he hoped was a teasing grin. "You could let me walk you home." He'd rushed on to introduce himself in case she didn't remember who he was. "After all, it's my job to see that the citizens are safe."

She'd given a low laugh that rivaled any music he'd heard. "I wouldn't want to interfere with your responsibilities."

So they walked together the few blocks.

She'd stopped before the house. "Thank you for protecting me against all the bad men." Her eyes had flashed with amusement.

Feeling rather pleased with his initial success in pursuing her, he'd pretended to be serious when he said, "Maybe you could return the favor by walking with me some evening."

She studied him under shy lashes, a smile teasing her lips. "I might consent to that."

"Good. Tonight at seven then?"

She laughed. Then nodded. "Very well." And with that, she'd hurried into the house.

He waited until the door closed behind her. He was about to turn away when he'd seen her peek from the window. He'd whistled as he sauntered away.

Why was he remembering the past? He had to deal with the present and the future. What future? What sort of life could he expect, apart from surviving winter in the mountains and exploring them in the summer? A smile curved his mouth as he thought of things he'd discovered. Caves of various sizes. A glacier he'd climbed. The water running from it so cold it made his chest hurt. He'd seen fields of alpine flowers. Watched mountain goats scale impossible cliffs and observed a grizzly bear playing with her cub.

He picked up the forgotten frozen towel, pressed it to his shoulder and studied his carvings.

The biggest, most life-like was the one he'd done of Mae. He glowered at it. It looked nothing like Mae. Its eyes were cold and expressionless. Its lips were immobile.

A groan escaped his lips. How he missed her smiling face. Like the time they'd gone to the Grand Union Hotel in Fort Benton for tea. High tea. Nothing like tea on the trail. The hotel had recently opened and it was grand enough to make a person's mouth drop open in awe. Heavy brocade drapes, high ceilings, the curved lobby desk, the wide gleaming wooden staircase. The dining room was so elegant that Austin swallowed hard. White linen tablecloths, gleaming crystal, and china. He swallowed again as they sat at one of the tables. Mae did not utter a sound from the time they entered until they were alone.

She'd leaned over and in a faint whisper said, "Austin, is this how the rich and famous live?"

He'd angled across the tabletop, afraid to speak aloud in the hushed atmosphere. "I've never been rich nor famous, so I can't say. But let's enjoy it."

A tier of delicacies was brought to them. For the price he'd paid, he expected something a little more robust, but it was fun to taste the different things. Besides, he hadn't come to eat, but to enjoy Mae's company.

She began to relax and look around. Their table was next to a window that overlooked the river and they watched the activity.

He remembered that was where she'd told him about her parents' death and coming west to live with her brother.

After that, she had begun to invite him into her home for a meal or a visit. Austin had never felt completely comfortable around Colin Senior. He assumed it was because he was a deputy sheriff and some people seemed to think that meant he was secretly looking for something he could arrest them for. Of course, that was the last thing on his mind when he was with Mae. All he'd wanted to do was be close to her.

Outside, snow slid from the roof and landed with a whomp.

Austin's shoulders rose and fell. He had to stop thinking of the past. His eyes narrowed. It was hard to, if not impossible, with the wooden likeness of Mae staring accusingly at him.

He didn't need it gaping sightlessly at him day and night. He got his ax and lifted it over Mae's wooden head. But he couldn't do it and returned the ax to its place.

He circled his tiny room. A chest-high shelf was full of things he'd carved. Mostly wildlife. There were several dogs. Had Colin found the note Austin had left with the dog the boy had carved? He'd made the words simple and short. *Sorry. I have to leave. Your dog is ready to give to your aunt. Take care of her for me.* Would Colin struggle trying to read it or give up and throw it away?

Carving had been one of the things that Austin had done to keep himself busy. That and reading.

He chose a piece of wood and sat at the table. But he stared at the far wall without doing anything. If he could carve something for Mae, he would be enthused. Well, why not? She might never get it, but he could still do it for her. A smile pulled his mouth upwards. He knew exactly what he'd make for her.

. . .

THE DAYS PASSED. One cold, snowy day after another. Always snow to move. Always cold to endure.

He paused before moving more snow. Was it this cold down at the Circle A Ranch? He looked in that direction, but of course, he could only see trees and mountains.

Were Mae and the children keeping warm? Who was making sure they were taken care of?

Because apart from God, John and Maude, Scottie and Leo, and six young couples, she was alone. He gave a bitter laugh. But knowing there were others to help her and make sure she was safe didn't make him feel any better. He wanted to be that person.

He returned to the cabin, warmed his hands and looked at the progress he'd made on his carving. But he didn't take it up. Instead, he prowled the square feet available to him.

If only he hadn't been the man to shoot Colin Senior. Though from their first meet, Austin had sensed the man wasn't living an honest life. Colin seemed suspicious about everything Austin said. His lack of trust was mutual. Austin knew it was only a matter of time before Colin would encounter trouble. He just wished someone else would be on the side of the law when that time came.

His thoughts swirled. His stomach felt sour.

He'd found comfort and strength in the scriptures

before and opened his Bible for the first time since he'd returned to the cabin.

The pages fell open to a well-used spot.

Romans chapter eight. The margins were stained and dog-eared from much reading. The familiar words filled his heart and mind. He read the chapter through. The last verse calmed his soul. *Nor height, nor depth, nor any other creature, shall be able to separate us from the love of God, which is in Christ Jesus our Lord.*

He might be alone and even lonely, but God was with him.

He closed the Bible and sighed. The snow had stopped. The sun was shining. Now would be a good time to bring in more wood. He banked the fire in the stove, put on his outerwear and left the cabin, taking his ax and saw with him. The first winter he'd stayed there, he'd made a sled for hauling stuff on and pulled it behind him into the woods.

There were some trees cut down that he'd meant to haul home before winter. But that plan had been sidetracked by finding Mae in need of his assistance.

He smiled as he sawed the logs into lengths he could put on his sled. The delay might have cost him having a good wood supply, but he didn't regret it one bit. In fact, he'd do the same thing again if he could and he broke into song as he dragged the loaded sled home.

That night, he again read that familiar chapter.

And we know that all things work together for good to them that love God, to them who are the called according to his purpose.

He wasn't sure what good had come of him shooting Colin Senior. It had twice cost him the woman he loved. Still loved with an ache that sucked at his innards. She'd never forgive him. Any more than he'd forgive himself. He didn't deserve to be around her. Could hardly stand to be around himself.

Oh, sure. For a few days, he'd allowed himself to push all those thoughts to the side. But he'd known from the beginning it was temporary.

Again and again, he went to the Bible, hoping for healing from the pain that tore at him until sometimes it was difficult to breathe. Often, he returned to the same chapter.

This evening, his eyes saw the first verse as if he'd never read it before. *There is therefore now no condemnation to them which are in Christ Jesus, who walk not after the flesh, but after the Spirit.*

No condemnation? That meant God would forgive him? Of course, He would. Why would Austin think otherwise?

"Dear God, I regret the things I've done. I'm sorry for shooting a man. Especially Mae's brother. Forgive me. And give Mae comfort. Keep her and the children safe."

He breathed in peace and joy. "Thank you, God."

The following days, his shoulder grew better, no longer paining him when he used it. But more importantly, his heart healed. He felt a lifting of the burden he'd carried five long years.

The days passed as he read from his Bible and carved the gift he had planned for Mae. And a plan began to emerge.

He looked at his calendar. He'd kept track of the days, more out of habit than a necessity to know what day it was or how many had passed since he'd last seen Mae. Those he counted with beats of his heart.

It was almost Christmas. He could make his way down the mountain. Deliver his presents without revealing himself. He could build a winter camp nearby and watch the ranch, maybe catching a glimpse of Mae and the children.

When he'd seen his fill, he'd return to his cabin. Not that he would ever get enough of seeing her, but if he thought she was happy and safe, he could be content.

It took all the next day to pack what he needed and secure what he left behind. The sun shone brightly. The weather looked good. And he began his journey down the mountain, singing loudly as he went. There was no one to hear him except the birds and they didn't seem to mind.

He arrived late in the day, the sun was already gone behind the mountains, leaving shadows to fill the scene. He drew to a halt to study the ranch. His gaze sought the schoolhouse. From his position, he could see the window over Mae's kitchen table. But there was no light glowing within the room. And every window of the schoolhouse was lit. Was something wrong?

His heart kicked into a gallop.

Dismissing his plan to stay out of sight, he rode to the school, swung to the ground, and burst through the door.

"You came back! I knew you would!" Colin shrieked and raced toward the man standing in the doorway.

Mae stared. She might have thought she was imagining it except for Colin's excitement and the way Rosie stood, her gaze riveted on Austin and her eyes brimming with happiness.

Mae couldn't take her eyes off the man either. His face was wrapped in a woolen scarf that appeared to have a layer of ice on it.

"I thought—" he mumbled.

"Get inside and close the door," John said and Austin did so. He uncoiled the scarf, allowing Mae a view of his whole face. He looked much the same which, for some reason, surprised her.

His gaze found hers across the room and he half-smiled. She saw the hesitancy in his eyes. It might be that she could fix that.

"You got here just in time." John's voice sounded far off.

Someone shoved a chair toward Austin and he sat.

Mae took a deep, calming breath and returned to presenting the program. "Children, are you ready?"

They nodded. The children had prepared the content of the program and she'd helped them smooth it out. Boyd, Gil, and Rosie, the three oldest, wanted to tell a memory from their first families.

Mae's eyes stung as Rosie told how her papa had made her a wooden horse big enough for her to ride on and then pulled her around on it all one afternoon.

Mae guessed there were other damp eyes as Boyd and Gil shared their memories. Boyd recalled a time when his pa had helped Boyd and Missy's ma do the dishes. "Mama's smile was something to see." He blinked furiously, then sat down.

Gil told a bit about his dead parents and then recalled when Tad began to walk. "Mama was holding his hands. She let go and Tad walked to me." His voice caught. "Mama said he liked me as much as her or Pa." He nodded. "Sure glad we got each other and now Yvette and Sam. Mama and Papa would be so happy."

The four younger students had decided to do the Christmas story and took turns reading out a simplified version of it while the others held up a picture book to illustrate.

Then they all sang 'Joy to the World.'

Had there ever been a more joyous occasion? Certainly, the remembrance of Christ's birth warranted rejoicing, but for Mae, so did Austin's arrival. She would tell him she forgave him before the evening ended.

But first, she passed out the booklets she'd made and gave the originals that she'd bound together with red yarn to Maude and John. The older couple clapped their hands and said how special the gift was.

"Why don't each of you come and give us a hug. And we have something for you."

The children each received a hug and a candy cane.

Mae's gaze went again and again to Austin. She couldn't wait to tell him what was on her heart. He met her gaze a few times and jerked away, but not before she glimpsed the uncertainty and regret in his eyes. She hoped to ease that latter before the day ended.

She'd never stopped loving him and could think of no greater joy than to let him know she didn't blame him for Colin Senior's death.

Scotty cleared his throat, a raspy sound. "Every one of ya come to the house. I've got snacks ready." He led the way out the door, then called over his shoulder. "Two horses out here needin' attention."

Austin was immediately on his feet. "I plumb forgot." He hurried for the door and then paused.

Mae thought he might have spoken to her, but the children pressed at his back, anxious for whatever Scottie had prepared for them.

"Take them to the barn," John called.

And Austin was pushed out of sight.

It didn't matter. She'd have time to tell him. Her thoughts stalled. Unless he wasn't staying. What if he'd only come for supplies and came by the ranch for a place to spend the night?

Rosie and Colin hung back from the others making their way across the yard.

"You two go along. I want to talk to Austin before I go over there." She handed them their coats.

Colin looked ready to argue. She understood he wanted to talk to Austin every bit as much as she did.

Rosie caught his hand. "Make sure he stays." She pulled Colin out the door. "The adults have to figure things out for themselves," she said to her brother.

Mae chuckled. Rosie might be more right than she could know.

She slipped into the living quarters, pulled on her warm coat and stepped out into the cold. The air was crisp and clear, the sky filled with thousands of twinkling stars. The sound of happy children and the murmur of adult conversation came from the big house, but for Mae, there was only one sound, one voice, she wanted to hear.

Light glowed from the barn and she crossed the snow-crunching path and slipped inside to where she knew she'd find Austin.

He carried a pack from off a horse. His eyes met hers and never left as he lowered it to the ground.

He straightened and stuck his hands into his coat pockets. "I never meant for you to see me. I was going to watch from a distance and make sure you were doing all right. Then ride on." He shrugged. "That was my plan. But when I saw lights on in the schoolroom, I thought something was wrong." He shrugged again. "Don't know what I was thinking."

He hadn't wanted to see her? "You were going to ride by without saying hello?" All her hopes that he still held some sweet regard for her vanished. She half-turned, preparing to leave him to his lonely choices. But he had to know she forgave him.

She moved to within a yard of him. "I'm glad you stopped. There's something I want to tell you."

His gaze darted to her face and away to something behind her.

As if he couldn't even bear to look at her. That knowledge combined with knowing he hadn't planned to stop and see her, ripped her heart in two.

However, she would not be deterred. She had prayed for this opportunity and it might be her last, so she lifted her chin and began. "Austin, I don't blame you for my brother's death. I believe you did what you had to do. Colin shouldn't have chosen the path he did and he paid for it."

Austin's gaze returned to her. His eyes filled with hope and doubt intermingled together.

She continued. "My only regret is that you didn't talk to me about it. You rode away, leaving me to deal with two losses. My brother and the man I love and whom I'd thought loved me."

He opened his mouth and closed it again. Swallowed audibly. "Mae, I—" Then nothing.

She'd hoped confessing her love would cause him to confess his love for her.

She spun around, then made it to the door and the cloak of darkness before tears escaped down her cheeks.

13

Austin stared after Mae. She forgave him. Understood. Her words eased the tension from his heart and he laughed softly.

Had she said she loved him? As in past tense or present? He couldn't be sure he'd heard her correctly.

He finished taking care of the horses and stepped from the barn.

The sound of laughter and conversation came from the house. He stood by the barn, uncertain if he should join the others. They'd make him welcome, but he might not be good company. He wanted to laugh for no other reason than Mae didn't blame him for Colin's death.

His laughter died. Could he ask her to repeat those other words? The ones about love.

The door opened and a young girl crossed the

veranda and trotted in his direction. Rosie. Sweet, little Rosie. She definitely lived up to her name. What was she doing out there?

She continued until she was close enough to see him. "I prayed you would come back."

"You did?"

"Because we need you."

"What for? There are lots of people around the place." He'd taken comfort in knowing they were never alone.

"None of them is you."

"Huh?" What did she mean by that?

"Couldn't we be a family?"

Rosie's words hit Austin like a physical blow. "You'd like that?"

"Very much and so would Colin."

He shouldn't have asked it, but the words came out anyway. "What about your aunt?"

He could make out Rosie's smile in the light of the moon. "She said she hoped you would come back."

"She had something to tell me, but now she has." Was that her only reason for wanting him to return? He hadn't had time to accept that she'd forgiven him. It was too much to hope for more.

"She doesn't want you to leave again."

"How do you know that?"

"Sometimes when she thinks I'm sleeping, I'm not.

Sometimes she prays out loud." Rosie looked up at him; her eyes wide and guileless.

"And what does she pray?" He shouldn't be asking a child to repeat things she heard at home. But he had to know.

Rosie leaned closer. "She asks God to hear the cry of her heart. I don't know what that means. But then she says something about loving you still and needing you."

He squeezed Rosie's shoulder. "Is that so?" His gaze went to the house. "Shall we join the others?"

They walked side by side to the house, Rosie's hand in his.

If he was to believe Rosie, Mae loved him. He loved her. His love had not changed in five years.

They joined the others in the kitchen. He forced himself to let his gaze circle the room, but then it came to Mae, and there it stayed. Until she lowered her gaze and her cheeks turned pink and he realized he was staring.

Colin took his other hand and led him to the table. The children helped him get a cup of hot cocoa and filled his plate with cookies and sweets. They sat together across the room from Mae. He couldn't stop himself from constantly looking at her.

"You're welcome to stay in one of the rooms upstairs," Maude said.

It took Austin a moment to realize she talked to

him. "That's very generous. But I don't mind staying in the bunkhouse again." He hadn't really planned to stay on the ranch at all. But if he was in the bunkhouse the kids...and maybe, Mae...could visit him. "If you don't mind."

Maude looked toward John. John smiled at his wife then turned to Austin. "You're more than welcome for as long as you like."

"Thanks."

"You're staying, aren't you?" Colin asked, the longing in his voice making Austin want to put down permanent roots immediately.

"We'll see." That was all he said, keeping his attention on his plate of food so he didn't look at Mae. He answered questions about life up the mountain. He listened to the others tell of their plans for the next few days leading up to Christmas and all the while, tried to come up with some way of finding an opportunity to speak to Mae.

Suddenly, everyone was leaving the house.

He was on his feet. Colin and Rosie put their coats on and waited for him to put on his. Mae was at the door. Her gaze went from the children to him and she shrugged.

He fell in at her side as they stepped from the veranda. The children dropped his hands and ran ahead, leaving him to escort Mae.

"This reminds me of the first time I walked you

home," he said, hoping to invite her to share her memories.

She chuckled. "As I recall you were only doing your duty as a deputy."

"As a deputy, I didn't walk all the young ladies home."

"Is that so?"

He tried to think if she sounded as if she liked the idea of him singling her out. "Seems I walked you home quite a few times after that."

"I guess you did." They reached the door and stopped. The children ran inside. Rosie gave Austin and Mae a nod and closed the door behind herself.

Austin had to say something while he had the chance. "Mae, I'm sorry I left you without an explanation. I couldn't forgive myself for what I'd done and didn't expect you would. Thank you for saying you do." He gulped in air and hurried on before she could speak. "I loved you so much, but couldn't bear the thought of hurting you the way I did. Mae, I have never stopped loving you."

They faced each other. Inches between them but five years separating them.

He pressed on. "If you still care about me, could we try again?"

"Austin, I have never stopped caring for you."

He pulled her into his arms and held her tight. His heart threatened to explode from his chest.

She sighed and leaned back to look up at him. "Do you know how many times I have longed for this?"

"Loving? Holding? Or maybe kissing?"

"Yes to all of them," she murmured.

He pressed his hands to either side of her head and held her like a fragile flower as he lowered his lips to hers. At first, their kiss was tentative, uncertain. It had been so long. Far too long.

Her lips warmed beneath his. She pressed her hands to the back of his neck and sighed.

He meant it to be a quick kiss but at her sigh, he held her closer and claimed her lips with a groan.

She eased back. "Austin, I have missed you so much."

"No more than I've missed you." There was so much he wanted to say.

The doorknob rattled.

She chuckled. "I think there are two children wondering if I'm ever coming in."

"I've got to get things organized to stay in the bunkhouse." Still, they stayed wrapped in each other's arms.

He lowered his arms. Reluctantly. Slowly. "I'll see you tomorrow."

"Come for breakfast."

"I'd love that." He gave her a quick kiss, then hurried away. He didn't stop until he was in the bunkhouse and before he lit the lamp, he looked out the window to see golden light glowing from Mae's home. A smile curving his lips and filling his heart, he lit the lamp then realized his belongings were still in the barn. He started a fire, jogged over to the barn for them. He paused before he stepped into the bunkhouse. Mae looked out the window.

Looking to see where he was.

The thought warmed him clear through.

Rosie and Colin tugged Mae's hands as soon as she stepped inside.

"What did you say to him?" Rosie asked.

"Is he staying forever?" Colin's tone indicated he would be satisfied with nothing less.

Mae felt as if her eyes glowed and her lips were rosy. But the children didn't seem to notice. "He's coming over for breakfast in the morning. You can ask him questions then, but remember your manners."

"We will," they chorused.

She knew it was pointless to expect them to settle after all the excitement of the evening. She wouldn't sleep either. "Let's take down the decorations in the schoolroom." She wasn't sure they would agree, but they did.

And they chattered. Mostly about Austin. Why had he come back? She let them answer their own questions. Because they'd prayed for it, but also because he missed them. How long was he staying? Colin figured forever, but Rosie looked at her aunt.

"I think it might depend on what you say."

Curious as to what Rosie meant, Mae asked what she expected her to do.

"You have to let him know you love him. Auntie Yvette and Auntie Grace both said so."

They'd been discussing Mae?

But Rosie hurried on. "They said sometimes people are afraid to say the words and then the other person doesn't know. And if they don't know, they might think it's because you don't care."

Mae hugged her niece. "I think you're right. Rest assured, I'm not afraid to tell him how I feel, but love is something you don't want to rush into." Though their love had grown slowly and deliciously back then and had survived fears of absence and uncertainty.

Rosie gave her a considering look. "But you loved him before. I remember."

"You do? You were only five."

"I saw him kiss you and I knew it meant you loved each other."

"Well!" She couldn't imagine where or when Rosie had seen them kissing. They'd been discreet, especially around the children.

Rosie nodded; her smile wide. "I liked watching you. It made me happy."

"That's nice." Would the child ever stop surprising her?

"I'd be happy again, you know." Rosie gave her aunt a pleading look.

"Me too," Colin said.

Mae laughed. "I'd be happy too, but first, let's enjoy breakfast with him tomorrow."

"And then Christmas."

She couldn't promise he'd stay for Christmas. But she could hope, seeing as it was only two days away.

They took down the decorations that adorned the room but left the chairs and desks where they were. They would have a Sunday service before classes resumed.

"Who wants to decorate our place?"

The children were eager to do so.

"Austin will like this, won't he?" Rosie asked as they hung the pretty paper chains along the wall.

"He sure will." Colin didn't give Mae a chance to answer.

Several times Mae glanced out the window. Seeing the light glowing in the bunkhouse window made her certain she wasn't imagining that Austin had returned and she smiled for no other reason than to know he was over there.

Tomorrow he was coming to share breakfast with them

She wondered if anyone in this house would sleep tonight.

Surprisingly, she slept soundly and wakened the next morning, more eager for the day than she'd been in a long time.

Maybe since Austin had left five years ago.

She'd made cinnamon rolls two days ago and there was enough left to share with Austin. There was bacon and eggs. She'd make pancakes as well. After all, this was a very special occasion.

But first, she had to tame her hair and she coiled it around her head and fixed it in place with a couple dozen hairpins. She put on a pink and purple flowered shirtwaist and a slim gray skirt. Standard teacher apparel, but at least the pink brought out the color in her cheeks. Not that they would likely need any help. Just thinking of Austin heated her cheeks. She put a matching pink apron on—her favorite—and began making breakfast.

The children were up and dressed and watching out the window.

"He's coming," they said.

Mae went to the window as if she needed to verify their words. Oh, but he looked good. A tall man. Filled out some now. He took long strides. Emotion threatened to overwhelm her as she remembered the way he had shortened his stride when they were together so she could keep up.

His head was bare, despite the cold. His brown hair was in need of a trim. The wind would have it mussed before he crossed the yard.

The children watched until he was almost there, then rushed to open the door.

She returned to the stove to save breakfast from burning.

Rosie and Colin pulled Austin inside.

He ruffled Colin's hair and patted Rosie. They hung on to him with both hands. He laughed. "Nice to see you both." His eyes, warm with emotion that she'd seen before, met hers and she was eighteen years old again, in love for the first time with the man who smiled at her from across the room.

"Good morning, Mae." His rich voice poured sweetness into her soul. How she'd missed the way his tone seemed to caress her.

"Morning to you." Did her voice sound as husky to him as it did to her?

He smiled. "Smells good in here."

"I suppose you're hungry," Rosie said. "Sit here while I set the table." She pulled him toward a chair.

While Rosie set the table and Mae tended the meal, Colin hung over the back of Austin's chair. His breath would be hot on Austin's neck, but the man didn't seem to mind.

"Are you glad to be back?" Colin demanded.

"I most certainly am."

"What didya do while you were gone?"

Mae thought of stopping Colin's questions, but she was anxious to hear the answers.

"I shoveled a heap of snow. I cut firewood. Read some. Carved some. Then I shoveled more snow and chopped more wood. Oh yeah, I cooked some meals."

"But you was all by yourself."

Austin pulled Colin forward to his knee. "I missed you too." He caught Rosie and pulled her to his side. "And you." He smiled at Mae. "And I missed you." His gaze captured Mae's and held her in an invisible embrace.

Her lungs had stalled.

"Are we gonna eat soon?" Colin asked.

Mae jerked around to the stove. The meal was ready. The coffee had boiled. She poured Austin and herself each a cupful and filled platters with eggs, bacon, and pancakes.

The four of them circled the table with the food before them.

"Austin, would you ask the blessing?"

He nodded. Did he remember the sweet times they had shared a meal and he'd offered the grace? They'd held hands as he prayed. She'd felt like they were united in a special way.

When he reached for her hand, a lump tightened

her throat. He did remember.

His fingers closed around hers, warm and strong. He took Colin's hand on the other side. The children held hands without any fuss and Mae took Rosie's hand. The lump in her throat grew so large she couldn't swallow.

Austin began, his voice deep and steady. "Dear God, You are so good to us. I am grateful for being with these people. You've given us a warm home and plenty of food and You've sent Your Son. We are blessed and we thank You. Amen."

Her hand lingered in his. Not until Rosie giggled did Mae pull away. "Let's eat."

Colin stared at Austin. "You said us."

"Pardon?" Austin looked confused.

"You said thanks for giving *us* a warm home. Us. That means you're staying."

"Colin, I—" Austin looked to Mae in silent appeal.

"Colin, take some pancakes and pass them on," Mae spoke gently, knowing the boy's dreams matched her own. But it wasn't a decision that they could rush Austin into.

She prompted the children to tell Austin what they were learning in school.

Rosie explained about the stories they'd given to John and Maude.

"It sounds like your plan worked out very well." He smiled at Mae.

All too soon the meal was over. Now he would leave. Hopefully only back to the bunkhouse.

But Rosie and Colin seemed set on delaying his departure. They brought out books and pictures to show him, had him tour the classroom as if he hadn't been there just a few hours ago.

Mae cleaned up the kitchen while they were in the classroom. And tried to think of ways to delay him.

The three of them returned, looking mighty pleased with themselves.

"Mae, would you like to go for a walk by the creek this afternoon? The children say they'd like to."

"I'd love to." She'd be happy to spend time with him anywhere. Doing anything.

"Good. Let me take care of my horses now."

"Can we come?" Colin gave him a beseeching look.

"If it's all right with your aunt."

"Of course." She was happy to see them so excited about his presence and his interest. But she'd be alone when they left. Alone to confront her dreams and fears.

Austin stopped in front of her. "Why don't you put on your coat and come with us?"

Laughing a little, she grabbed her coat. The four of them crossed the yard to the barn.

The children followed Austin from one horse to the other, from the feed bin back to each horse while Mae stood to one side watching.

Austin's gaze came to her so often, his eyes full of promise. Her cheeks were continually warm, her heart continuously thumping hard. He teased the children, making them giggle.

Mae laughed at their play. In fact, she couldn't remember when she'd laughed so much. For the first time in years, the world was full of sweet wonder.

"Let's take that walk now," Austin said, and they went from the barn down to the river. The children alternately ran and played and then returned to walk beside Austin and Mae. They wandered aimlessly. Happy to be together. The children found amazing things, like the shape the ice had made along the bank. The most amazing thing for Mae was having Austin at her side, the strain of the last few weeks removed.

As they returned home, Rosie turned to them. "This is like a real family," she said.

Austin stopped. "What do you mean?"

Colin came to Rosie's side, as if the pair had discussed this and were in agreement. "A mother and father who love each other and love the children." She waved in the general direction of the homes of the others. "Like them."

Mae choked up.

Austin turned slowly to face Mae. His smile promised everything she'd ever wanted— had ever once dreamed was possible.

"Is it too soon?" he asked.

"For what?"

He caught her hands. "Mae, I once asked you to marry me, but before you could answer—"

"As I recall, we were waiting for you to get permission from my brother." Her voice quivered as she understood his intent.

He turned to Colin and Rosie. "Do I have your permission to ask your aunt to marry me?"

"Yes. Yes." Rosie clapped and Colin jumped up and down.

Her hands still in his, he faced her. "Mae Martyn, I love you with my whole heart. Now and forever. Will you marry me?" Before she could answer, he continued. "If you do, I promise I will never leave you again so long as I live. At least never willingly."

That was enough for her. "Austin Wagoner, I love you more than words can say, and yes, I'll marry you."

"Kiss her," Rosie said.

They kissed, a chaste, quick kiss, then Austin hugged her, lifting her off her feet to swing her around.

"I love you." He set her down and pulled the children to his side, hugging them. "I love both of you too."

The world shone with a thousand lights as they made their way back to Mae's place. Austin spent the day with them, not leaving until after the evening meal.

"I have to go now."

The children nodded.

"It's all right if Auntie Mae goes out with you." Rosie blushed, informing both Austin and Mae that she meant so they could kiss goodnight.

Austin planted a kiss on the girl's head. "You are a real sweetheart."

She blushed even more.

Austin waited while Mae got her coat and went outside with him.

He drew her to his chest and whispered in her ear. "Do you think they are listening at the door?"

Whispering provided the perfect excuse to press her mouth to his ear. "I know they are."

"Mae, I love you. I will never get tired of telling you that."

"I will never get tired of hearing it. I love you too."

His arms tightened around her. "I regret those wasted years."

She did too, but she didn't want the past standing between them in any way. "Austin, the past is over and done with. Any mistakes or misunderstandings are gone. The only thing between us is forgiveness."

He pressed his cheek to her head. "You are so kind and generous. Is it any wonder I love you so much?"

She tipped her face to him. He claimed her lips in a kiss so full of love and promise that her chest could barely contain her swelling heart.

14

The next day was Christmas and the children were up before dawn. They dressed hurriedly and then pressed their noses to the window. Their breath froze to the glass and they scraped it away.

"His light is on. Why doesn't he come?" Colin demanded.

"Maybe he doesn't know we're awake." Rosie turned to Mae. "Auntie, put the lamp on the table so he can see it."

Mae, every bit as excited and impatient as the children, did so. She laughed for no other reason than the lamp in the bunkhouse was extinguished and seconds later, Austin stepped into the pre-dawn grayness.

"He's got a big sack." Colin's voice rounded with awe.

"Must be gifts." Rosie sat back. "We didn't make

him anything." She scampered to the bedroom and returned with the booklet of stories. "I'll give him this."

"What am I gonna give him?"

Rosie put her arm around her younger brother. "It's from both of us."

Mae cleared her throat before she could speak. "Rosie, that's very kind."

"He's here," Colin shouted and rushed to open the door.

Austin stepped inside.

As far as Mae was concerned, Christmas had arrived. She had all she wanted right here in this room.

Austin set his gunny sack down and held out his arms to the children. They rushed to him, getting hugged and tickled.

He met Mae's gaze over the children and tipped his head. "Join us."

She didn't need to be asked twice. In fact, she probably didn't need to be asked even once. She had five years to make up for. His arms opened up to include her. He leaned forward to give her a quick kiss.

Colin, squeezed between them, squirmed. Laughing, they broke apart.

"I need to make breakfast," Mae said.

"What's in your bag?" Colin stared at the bulky sack by the door.

"Gifts. Can we see them before breakfast?" Austin looked at Mae, his eyes pleading as much as Colin's.

Mae laughed. "Why not? After all, it's Christmas."

They sat in a circle as Austin opened the sack. He pulled out two little parcels wrapped in brown store paper and handed one to each of the children.

Rosie simply held the package, awe and joy wreathing her face.

Mae reached for Austin's hand and held it tight. He had brought so much happiness into this home.

Colin ripped the paper off to reveal a finely-carved horse. "Thanks."

Rosie slowly folded back the paper on her gifts. It was a carved kitten looking so real Mae was tempted to pet it.

Rosie clutched it to her chest. "Thank you. I will love it forever."

The children's attention returned to the bulging sack.

Mae had to admit her curiosity was alive and well.

Austin shifted so he faced Mae full on. "I thought of you so much. I had the wooden statue I carved that looked a tiny bit like you, but it was wooden, lifeless. I almost destroyed it. Instead, I put my energies into making something I thought you would like." He hesitated, as if having second thoughts.

She cupped her hand to his cheek. "Austin, anything you made for me will be special."

He nodded, his eyes warm with affection. He drew out an object.

"It's a manger," he said as he handed it to her. "There's more." He pulled out the figure of a woman in a long robe and then a man in a long coat. Then a baby. He set them up. The baby in a manger with the adult figures watching over the baby.

"It's Mary and Joseph," Colin said.

"And Baby Jesus." Rosie's voice was full of wonder.

Mae didn't wait for Austin to return his gaze to her. She leaned forward and kissed him.

Colin groaned.

Austin laughed. "You better get used to it."

"You're going to kiss her all the time, aren't you?" Rosie seemed to think it was a good thing.

"I sure am. All the time." He kissed Mae again, then sat back. "I have something else for you." He dug in his pocket.

Mae stared at the golden locket in his palm. Speechless, she lifted her gaze to his.

"I found it after the robbery. It must have fallen from your bag."

"I thought I'd lost it." Tears in the back of her throat made it hard to talk.

He undid the clasp and held up the ends.

She turned and let him fasten the chain around her neck. He kissed her cheek as she pressed the little heart to her chest.

Rosie reached for the little booklet and handed it to Austin. "This is from Colin and me."

Austin turned the pages. "Thank you. I will cherish this forever." He caught the two children in his arms. "But I'll cherish the two of you even more."

Mae's heart overflowed with joy.

But she hadn't forgotten her gift for Austin and slipped into the bedroom. She returned with a pair of warm woolen socks she'd knitted in the evenings. As evidence to herself that she believed he would return.

"I made these for you."

"Thank you." He examined them, his expression puzzled. "But how did you know I was coming back?"

"'Cause we prayed." Colin's voice was loud with enthusiasm.

Mae nodded. "I reasoned that if our love had survived five years, it was strong enough to pull you back to us."

"I didn't know—" He didn't finish. Words about shooting Colin Senior would never be spoken in front of the children.

Mae pressed her fingertips to Austin's lips. "The past is past. Let's leave it there and celebrate the present."

"I'd like that."

She handed the children the presents she'd prepared for them. Rosie was thrilled to have her mother's combs and Colin donned his father's hat with pride.

Mae clung to Austin's hand as emotion choked her.

"I'm hungry," Colin complained.

Laughing, Mae got to her feet and held out a hand to pull Austin up. Instead, he tugged her down, kissed her thoroughly, then let her go and rose on his own.

Sure that her cheeks were stained red, Mae hurried to the stove, Austin's laughter following her.

He joined her and together they made a hearty breakfast, though it might have taken more time than one would expect, as he often interrupted her to give her a kiss.

Later, they went to John and Maude's house to join the others for a big Christmas dinner.

As soon as they entered the kitchen, Colin shouted. "Guess what. Auntie Mae and Austin are going to get married! They love each other!" He paused long enough to draw in more air. "They kiss a lot."

The others laughed and clapped and offered congratulations.

Mae wondered if her hot cheeks would be permanently bright red.

EPILOGUE

The day had finally come. There had been times Austin wondered if it ever would.

John had invited Austin to visit him at the sitting room a few days after Christmas.

"I once offered you a place on the ranch. We could use another man. Are you interested now?"

"I'm interested, but I'd have to discuss it with Mae."

"Very wise of you. I hope she agrees. It would provide us with a teacher. At least until babies come along and take up her time."

Babies! Not that Austin hadn't thought of it. Rosie would make a wonderful big sister. Colin would be good with younger siblings too.

He and Mae had discussed John's offer.

"It would be wonderful to have a permanent home," Mae said.

Austin was now part of the Circle A Ranch. He'd wondered if the six men who had spent years on the place would object to him joining them, but he was warmly welcomed by one and all.

Then there had been the matter of a place to live. Both Austin and Mae said they would be content to live in the teacher's quarters. They didn't mind being crowded, but John and Maude both insisted that wasn't necessary.

"You're welcome to live in the teacher's quarters as long as Mae is teaching, of course. But it needs to be bigger."

And so began a building project.

"I'm sorry to be the cause of you all having to work in the cold of winter," he said to the men. Two of them took turns staying to work on the addition while the others herded cows.

Sam was one of those who had stayed behind when Austin apologized. "Nonsense. We're grateful for a reason to be with our wives."

The addition consisted of three bedrooms. The room Mae and Rosie now shared would become a sitting room.

The work was reduced to a few hours a day when school resumed. And in order to allow for more construction, Mae, with the approval of all concerned, had shortened the school day.

. . .

THE CONSTRUCTION WAS COMPLETE. And today, Mae and Austin were to become husband and wife.

Austin straightened the tie John had given him.

A preacher had come out from the fort to conduct the ceremony.

They were to be married in the classroom. How fitting, Austin decided.

The only guests and witnesses were those who lived at the ranch. After the ceremony, a feast had been prepared for them at the big house.

Austin was ready and made his way to the school. Colin had been watching for him and they met at the front of the room, the others seated behind them.

"How do I look?" Colin whispered.

Austin took in the white shirt and black string tie. "Perfect." He squeezed the boy's shoulder.

The adjoining door opened and Rosie stepped out, beautiful in a pink dress with her hair swept up in a bunch of ringlets.

She made her way to Austin's left.

And then Mae stood framed in the doorway and Austin saw nothing else.

She too wore a pink dress. The color reflected in her cheeks. Her hair hung down her back in curls. He had never seen it down and was amazed at the massive gold fall.

She met his gaze. And never once wavered from

looking at him as she came to his side and took his elbow.

He heard the words of the preacher as if from a hollow tube. He must have answered the questions correctly because the preacher announced that they were husband and wife.

"You may kiss your bride."

Mae pressed her hands to his shoulders and lifted her face to receive his kiss.

"They're always kissing," Colin announced to the others.

Rosie watched, approval in her eyes, then she faced the gathering. "We're all going to be very happy."

Austin and Mae turned. He nodded. "I couldn't have said it any better than Rosie has. We are very happy."

They marched out the door and across to the other house, the others clapping and cheering them on.

Mae's eyes glowed. "I love you, Austin Wagoner."

He pulled her close. "I love you, Mae Wagoner."

The children joined them. "When are we going to be Wagoners?" Rosie asked.

"Yeah," Colin echoed.

Austin and Mae had discussed adopting the children but weren't sure if the children would want that. It seemed they would.

"If that's what you want, we'll make arrangements," Mae said.

"Then we'll be really truly family," Rosie said. "And live happily ever after."

"Amen," Austin said.

ALSO BY LINDA FORD

Historical Romance

Love on the Western Trail

Renewed Love

Rescued Love

Reluctant Love

Redeemed Love

Romancing the West

Jake's Honor

Cash's Promise

Blaze's Hope

Levi's Blessing

A Heart's Yearning

A Heart's Blessing

A Heart's Delight

A Heart's Promise

Sunny Ridge, Montana

Rodeo and Juliet

Glory, Montana

Loving a Rebel

A Love to Cherish

Renewing Love

A Love to Have and Hold

Cowboy Father

Cowboy Groom

Cowboy Preacher

Rancher's Bride

Hunter's Bride

Christmas Bride

Love on the Santa Fe Trail

Wagon Train Baby

Wagon Train Wedding

Wagon Train Matchmaker

Wagon Train Christmas

Dakota Brides series

Temporary Bride

Abandoned Bride

Second-Chance Bride

Reluctant Bride

War Brides series

Lizzie

Maryelle

Irene

Grace

Wild Rose Country

Crane's Bride

Hannah's Dream

Chastity's Angel

Cowboy Bodyguard

Contemporary Romance

Montana Skies series

Cry of My Heart

Forever in My Heart

Everlasting Love

Inheritance of Love

Copyright © 2020 by Linda Ford

All rights reserved.

No part of this book may be reproduced in any form or by any electronic or mechanical means, including information storage and retrieval systems, without written permission from the author, except for the use of brief quotations in a book review.

Made in the USA
Coppell, TX
25 March 2025

47532493R00146